"Not sure of this?" he murmured.

"You too? I'm afraid we've invited a disaster on each other."

"Yeah. I saw their expressions. Well…we'll re-trade around six-thirty?"

"Sounds right. I'll bring Paul earlier if there's any problem or he wants to go home." She lifted a hand.

He got it, she wanted to touch-knuckles. They were, after all, in this project together. So he leaned forward to touch her knuckles, and again, she looked straight at him.

Just like that, it happened again. A wildfire of emotion, torching through his veins. Need, coiling like a snake. Wanting, whispering like silk through his witless mind.

If their sons would just go along with their crazy plan, he'd have chances to see her again. To be around her. To see if she ever peeled off that careful, friendly veneer for a man…or if she could be coaxed to.

Dear Reader,

I love writing stories about a man and a woman who are positive they couldn't possibly end up together. She knows it can't happen. He knows it can't happen. But then comes love…and all their preconceptions are blown to smithereens.

Although this kind of story is always fun…behind the scenes, I believe it touches on something very serious and true. There is no perfect time to fall in love—no convenient time to find the right mate. The more challenging the circumstances, the more two people have to conquer obstacles in their path, and the more tested and strong their love will be.

In this case, I added two boys—partly because I love writing children characters—but also because kids are brilliant at throwing obstacles in their parent's way. Of course, *they* think they're helping.…

Hope you enjoy!

Jennifer Greene

www.jennifergreene.com

LITTLE MATCHMAKERS

JENNIFER GREENE

Recycling programs
for this product may
not exist in your area.

ISBN-13: 978-0-373-65684-4

LITTLE MATCHMAKERS

www.Harlequin.com

Printed in U.S.A.

Books by Jennifer Greene

Harlequin Special Edition

The 200% Wife #1111
The Billionaire's Handler #2081
Yours, Mine & Ours #2108
Little Matchmakers #2202

Silhouette Romantic Suspense

Secrets #221
Devil's Night #305
Broken Blossom #345
Pink Topaz #418
§*Secretive Stranger* #1605
§*Mesmerizing Stranger* #1626
§*Irresistible Stranger* #1637

Silhouette Desire

***Prince Charming's Child* #1225
***Kiss Your Prince Charming* #1245
†*Rock Solid* #1316
Millionaire M.D. #1340
††*Wild in the Field* #1545
††*Wild in the Moonlight* #1588
††*Wild in the Moment* #1622
Hot to the Touch #1670
The Soon-to-Be-Disinherited Wife #1731

Silhouette Books

Birds, Bees and Babies
   "Riley's Baby"
Santa's Little Helpers
   "Twelfth Night"

***Happily Ever After*
†*Body & Soul*
††*The Scent of Lavender*
§*New Man in Town*

JENNIFER GREENE

lives near Lake Michigan with her husband and an assorted menagerie of pets. Michigan State University has honored her as an outstanding woman graduate for her work with women on campus. Jennifer has written more than seventy love stories, for which she has won numerous awards, including four RITA® Awards from the Romance Writers of America and their Hall of Fame and Lifetime Achievement Awards.

You're welcome to contact Jennifer through her website at www.jennifergreene.com.

To Cathie, Jimmie, Susan, Suzette, Julie & Margaret.
You know why! Love you all!

Chapter One

Tucker MacKinnon took the sharp curves of Whisper Mountain at daredevil speeds. Typical of a June morning in South Carolina, the sun burned hotter than a bad temper and the humidity was claustrophobic.

His mood was just as miserable.

Anyone in the MacKinnon family could testify that Tucker had never owned a temper. He was the go-to guy in a tornado. He'd handled rattlers and black bears. Hell, he'd made a career of handling people no one else could get along with—kids with attitude, adults in trouble, personnel wars in small companies. Those challenges were downright fun. But not this.

Nothing was fun about this.

He braked for a stop sign at the base of the mountain, and then it was only a skip and a jump to the elementary school parking lot. His stomach immediately began pitching nerves. Today was the last day of school, as witnessed by the squalling behavior of honking cars and chattering parents. He had to scramble to find a parking spot. Kids were leaping and shrieking as they bounded out the door, free for the summer…except for the few hanging tight in the school entrance.

Those few kids had been singled out. They weren't allowed to get their report cards until a parent talked to their child's teacher.

Tucker's ten-year-old son was one of those hovering in the doorway…until he spotted the familiar silver truck, and then he galloped straight for his dad. Will had his father's genetic build, which pretty much meant he came out of the womb looking like a beanpole, long and lean. For certain he was the tallest kid in elementary school, but right now, his usually sun-brushed skin was pale, his first words gushing from a pent-up dam.

"I didn't do anything, Dad. Honest. Whatever Mrs. Riddle says, it wasn't me. It couldn't have been me. I don't even know what it's about."

"Hey." Tucker cuffed an arm around his son's neck. "Would you quit worrying? Whatever it is, we'll fix it."

"I keep trying to think what I did wrong. I've been racking and racking my brain. I can't always answer her questions, so maybe that's it. But she never calls on me when I raise my hand. She only calls me when I don't. I mean, how could she be mad at me about *that?*"

Tucker had no idea why the infamous Mrs. Riddle had held back Will's report card, but he was hoping— for her sake—that she had a damned good reason. He walked into the cool, dim hall, and felt his stomach churn another stress ball. Everyone in the MacKinnon family was a major academic achiever except for him. He'd never liked grade school. Or middle school. Come to think of it, he'd never liked school altogether—and schools had never much liked him. He was thirty-one now, of course. Only two things really mattered to him in life. His work on Whisper Mountain.

And above everything else, a hundred times over, was his son.

Mrs. Riddle had better not be unfairly picking on his son, or some major fur was going to fly.

"How about if you just hang by your old locker? Stay inside where it's cool. And you'll be able to hear me if I call."

Will slumped off, and Tucker rounded the corner and trekked down the long hall to the last classroom. Not that Mrs. Riddle had a reputation for being a sharp-nosed martinet, but all the other teachers had ditched the place as fast as the kids. Her doorway was the only one with a pair of parents still waiting.

Right off, Tucker recognized the woman just ahead of him.

She was Petie's mom.

He could only see the back of her. Didn't matter. A bad marriage was supposed to cure a guy of believing in hopeless causes. Didn't matter. His son was and needed to be his whole world right now.

For darn sure, *that* mattered. But that didn't stop a guy from admiring the view.

Her hair—the color of lush dark honey, ribboned with sun streaks—swayed past her shoulders. He'd often seen her in the same "uniform"—a yellow polo shirt with dark green shorts. The top had a Plain Vanilla logo over the pocket. It was the name of her store, a fresh spice and herb shop tucked in a curve of Whisper Mountain. By any logic, the shop should have failed; the location was obscure, and who'd travel out of their way for a spice or two?

His opinion, not for the first time, had proven dead wrong. Everyone on Whisper Mountain knew the place, shopped there, heaped praise on her for what she was doing.

Tucker wouldn't know tarragon from paprika, but that wasn't to say he didn't appreciate spice. The fit of her shorts, for example. The shape snugged over the cup of her fanny, and led straight down to unforgettable thighs and calves. She worked outside and it showed, from the sun-golden tint of her skin to her trim, tight body.

She had a major flaw, seeing that she was as short as a shrimp. He doubted she could reach five-three unless she was standing on a rock.

The rest of the package intrigued him every time he saw her. She was…interesting. Natural, earthy. No pretensions to her. Sensual.

A parent left Mrs. Riddle's classroom—a mom, flush-faced and exiting at a fast jog. Petie's mom drew a breath, and then headed into the classroom to brave the dragon, leaving him still thinking about her.

Her name was Garnet. Garnet Cattrell. She'd captured his attention last September, the first day of school, but he never seemed to capture hers. She always answered a "hi" with a "hi" back and a smile, but two seconds after initiating conversation with her, she always found a way to move off.

She wasn't unfriendly exactly. It was more like… she didn't see him. He could have been a lamppost. A brother. A catalog in the mail. An entity that was easily ignorable.

Naturally, Tucker had backed off. He was in no hustle to make any more mistakes with the female gender. Maybe she didn't like six-three guys with blue eyes.

Maybe she had an allergy to size-fourteen feet. Maybe his voice was too low, or his hands too calloused.

Whatever.

The only thing that mattered right now was her being here. Because if *her* kid had a problem with Mrs. Riddle, it must be time to start counting animals and climb on the ark. Armageddon couldn't be far down the road.

Tucker leaned back against the cool cement wall, not planning on eavesdropping, but damn. It was so easy. Voices carried through the open door. Mrs. Riddle's voice had a high nasal quality. Garnet's—like the gem—had a rich, quiet softness to it.

"I can't imagine what problem you could have with my Pete. As far as I know, he's been getting all As—"

"Of course he is. He's a very bright boy. I'm going to miss having him in my classroom," Mrs. Riddle said stridently. "But I've called in all those parents who, I believe, need some guidance. Middle school is not an easy transition for some children. There are things you might try over the summer to help Peter adjust more comfortably."

Tucker couldn't hear—or see—Garnet bristle. But for the first time, he heard something stiff and testy in her voice. "Do you have some reason to think Peter won't do perfectly fine in middle school?"

"I think he'll do perfectly fine academically. But possibly not socially. Peter is an academic," Mrs. Riddle said authoritatively. "But he's left out whenever it comes to sports. Nor does he ever 'hang out,' as they say, with a male peer group."

"But…he seems to get along with other kids. He's never mentioned a problem with anyone. He just isn't a highly social kid."

"He's an old soul," Mrs. Riddle explained. "And his

nature is on the quiet side. I understand all that. But I suspect you have quite a time getting his nose out of a book, or off the computer."

Tucker heard nothing for a minute. Then Garnet again. "That's true. But it's not as if I haven't encouraged him—"

"Mrs. Cattrell. I'm not criticizing you. And you can take my advice or leave it. But I strongly suggest that you use the summer to find some outdoor or athletic activity that he might like. Give him the opportunity to develop a skill in something outside the academic arena. It doesn't matter which sport. The issue is widening his world, giving him confidence. Kids can become merciless in middle school. You don't want Peter singled out."

They talked for a few more minutes. Not long. When Garnet strode from the classroom...Tucker would have talked to her, said something. But she moved past as if not seeing him or anything else, her expression looking something like a kicked puppy. Stricken. Hurt. Worried.

And then, of course, it was his turn to get beat up.

Mrs. Riddle was holding court from behind a desk older than sin—the elementary school was less than ten years old, so she must have brought the scarred-up thing with her. Her hair was steel-colored, springy, her eyes a gray-blue, like flint. Nobody messed with Mrs. Riddle.

She started right in with the stick-up-the-behind tone of voice. "Mr. MacKinnon. For once, your Will had a decent semester."

"All homework in on time. Studied for tests. Kept his nose clean."

"Yes. Well, we won't go so far as to call Will a saint, now, will we? But he's a good boy. The other children all like him, particularly the boys. He's a fine young athlete. I've enjoyed having him in my classroom. If

I needed help with anything, I could always count on Will to volunteer."

"Well…good." Tucker scratched behind an ear. He wasn't about to relax, but if all she was going to report was good news, he was even more confused why he'd been summoned in here.

"But here is the issue, Mr. MacKinnon. Will is going to enter middle school next year. And he has much more physical maturity than most boys his age. If he hasn't noticed girls already, he certainly will soon."

Tucker was still waiting for a headline. No news so far.

"Let me be frank, Mr. MacKinnon. I don't know your situation, as far as Will's mother, but I believe he seriously needs a helpful female influence."

"Wait. Why?"

"Because he's become afraid of girls. He turns beet-red when any of the girls talk to him. He walks into walls. He stumbles over his own feet. At the start of the school year, he was fine. But I believe some hormones have caught up with him at this point."

"Well, yeah. I'm sure they have. But…"

"You work primarily with men, don't you, Mr. MacKinnon? Men. Or boys. There are very few women in your business."

"That's true. But it's not because I planned it that way," Tucker said defensively. "It's just that the nature of my retreat and adventure programs seem to appeal more to males than females. And it's not as if there's never a woman around—"

"Women who Will has frequent occasions to talk with? I don't mean family. I mean women, where he's had the opportunity to form some sort of relationship, even if it's only casual."

"Well, sure he has." He hesitated. "I think. Well, maybe not."

"I thought not. So my suggestion to you, over the summer, is to arrange some activities where Will is more exposed to some female presence. A sport that both genders play. Chores where both genders are involved. Something to ease that nervousness he feels around females."

"Is he that way with you?"

Mrs. Riddle sighed, raising her eyes to the ceiling. "Mr. MacKinnon. Do I strike you as the nature of woman who would make an adolescent boy stutter?"

Tucker readily recognized there was no possible way he could answer that. Admitting she looked like an army tank didn't seem the right thing to mention. She ruled with an iron hand. Kids came out of her class thrilled to be free—but by reputation, they all considered they learned the most from her compared to the "easy" teachers. Anyway…he had to admit he understood what her concern with Will was about.

Tucker abruptly recalled the last time they'd stopped for burgers and fries. Will had tripped over a chair looking at a pigtailed tween on the other side of the room. So yeah. The kid had turned into a bumbler with girls.

Tucker got his son's report card and clipped out of the classroom, feeling edgy and frustrated. How was a father supposed to fix something like *that?* Sure, Will had a shy side with girls. But he was ten. Every boy had a bumbling stage around girls when they started adolescence.

Still, there was a nick of truth that bugged him. Will really didn't get exposed to many females, because of their lives, and Tucker's job, and where they lived. That never seemed to matter before. Will was a happy kid.

Now, though, Tucker could see how a guy-dominated environment could add up for Will—particularly since the only relevant female in his life, his mother, was hardly a role model.

Still…how to approach this topic with his son? And what would he tell Will about the meeting with his teacher?

He whipped around the corner—and charged smack into someone leaning against the wall. Or…not someone. Her. Petie's mom. Garnet.

While Pete needed a stop in the boy's bathroom, Garnet leaned against the cool wall and closed her eyes. She replayed every second of her conversation with Mrs. Riddle. Then did it all over again.

The lump in her throat refused to disappear.

She'd always been a marshmallow. A soft, peace-loving marshmallow. Confrontations always gave her nightmares.

Still, where her son was concerned, Garnet could change from happy wallflower into riled-up mama porcupine in two seconds flat. Nobody hurt her son. It was hard for her to hear even the smallest criticism of Petie for the obvious reason.

He wasn't just the best thing in her life. He was the best kid in the entire universe.

For Mrs. Riddle's sake, the teacher was lucky she hadn't picked on Petie.

Instead, she'd picked on Garnet.

Normally Garnet was braced for criticism. Lots of people had found fault with her—particularly in her own family. Lots of people claimed she'd disappointed them. But *no one* had ever suggested that she wasn't a good mother. At least before today.

Garnet still had the lump in her throat, the stab in her heart. Mrs. Riddle hadn't exactly said that she was an inadequate mom, but she'd implied it. A boy needed male role models. She'd failed to provide them. And that didn't bite just because the teacher said it. It bit because Garnet had worried about the same darn thing for eons now.

Absently she lifted a hand and immediately discovered a ragged cuticle.

Dang it. She loved working with dirt. Dirt, herbs, spices, flowers, plants of all kinds. But she always wore gloves when she was working outside—not because she was vain about her hands, but because of this. The instant a nail split, or a cuticle got ragged, she couldn't stand it. She had to fix it. She couldn't *think* with a frayed cuticle.

She was just biting the offending cuticle when a Mack truck ran into her.

The air whooshed out of her lungs. Her head hit the cement wall at the same time the Mack truck tire connected with her foot…the vulnerable, naked foot in the green Teva sandals.

"Aw, hell. Aw, hell. I'm really sorry. I wasn't looking—are you all right?"

If she were unconscious and in a coma, she'd have recognized that low, wicked baritone. Tucker. Tucker MacKinnon.

It just wasn't fair. Being hit with a real Mack truck, she could have coped with. Freight train, no problem. Bulldozer, ditto. Anything or anyone but Tucker.

He was undoubtedly trying to help, by steadying her, then rushing his hands down her arms, his gaze searching, seeking any injuries. She certainly had some. The back of her head was gushing something warm and wet, and so was her right foot.

None of the injuries were lethal. She was just going to be stuck with a couple of bruises. He was big; she was small. That was the total equation. It's just that if she had to have an accident, she wished it could have happened with anything but Tucker. Anyone but Tucker.

"I'm fine," she said. Although temporarily she was pretty sure her right foot was broken in fifty or sixty places.

"You can't be fine. You're not fine. Damn. The back of your head's getting a goose egg, and there's blood."

Undoubtedly. She'd scraped her head against the cement wall. Something had to give, and it hadn't been the wall.

"Let me see." His eyes were suddenly close enough for her to experience that electric-blue color close up. "The school's so deserted I just wasn't expecting anyone to be there. I was waiting for my son, thinking, not looking where I was going. Listen—"

After checking out her head, his hands cuffed her shoulders again. He was still squinting. Still searching for injuries. She was still dying, but more from embarrassment by then, particularly when he hunkered down.

"Broke your big toenail." He winced in sympathy. "Just hope I didn't break a toe. Or two."

He had. But who cared? Once the football hero of the county—there was no one in the county who didn't know the MacKinnon name—and he was kneeling at her feet. "I'm sure you didn't."

"How about if you just sit down right here, in the hall. I'll run into the office. They have to have some Band-Aids and first-aid supplies around here." Again, he tilted her head, not to look for injuries this time. He met her eyes. "Garnet, I couldn't be sorrier."

"It's okay. Honestly. Don't bother. I've got first-aid stuff at home."

He'd always made her nervous. It wasn't his fault, nothing he did. It was her. She'd always felt goofy around him. Drawing attention to herself over a hurt only made it worse.

"Nonsense. You don't want to trail blood into your car. And I think we should get some ice on your head. Just hold up. I'll be back in two shakes."

He'd barely taken three strides before Pete charged out of the boy's bathroom, saw her and sprinted over. He seemed to recognize Tucker as an afterthought, and immediately frowned. "Mr. MacKinnon. Did you hurt my mom?"

"No, Pete. Well, yes. I mean, I did, but it wasn't intentional—"

"Pete, I'm totally okay."

Pete, even if he was built on the small side, could turn more protective than a marine. He pushed his round glasses higher on his nose and faced Tucker. "*Why* would you hurt my mom? What happened?"

The commotion must have been heard from a distance, because from the office hall, Tucker's tall son suddenly charged into view. "Dad. Hey. What's going on. Mrs. Cattrell, how come you're bleeding?"

"Your dad hurt my mom," Petie informed him.

Will's jaw dropped. "No way."

"Just look at my mom if you don't believe me. She's bleeding all over the place."

"But my dad would never do anything like that. That's dumb."

Tucker had to raise his voice to be heard. "Boys.

Both of you. Go to the office. Ask for a first-aid kit and an ice pack."

Both boys laid out an "okay" and galloped together down the side hall, looking a lot like Mutt and Jeff. Garnet wanted to echo again that she was fine, and just wanted to go *home,* but it was like arguing with a freight train.

Tucker hunkered down again. "I know. You're going to live. But it won't kill you to have those two places disinfected and covered up."

"I know. I just hate—"

His tone changed, turned quieter. "Garnet. I heard what Mrs. Riddle said about your Petie. And this is obviously a poor time to pursue the subject. But I think we might both benefit from talking together."

"Talk about…?"

"My Will. Your Pete." He hesitated. "It's probably easier for me to get away than you. I could steal an hour around seven tonight. You free then?"

Free was a relative word. Like the song said, freedom was just another word for nothing left to lose, and looking at Tucker, Garnet knew perfectly well that she had a ton to lose by spending any time with him. Her dignity…although she'd already lost most of that, by bleeding all over the school hall. Her pride…though, she still had her pride. Something she'd guarded tighter than gold for the last few years.

"I just want to talk about the boys," he said. "A half hour? Your place?"

The boys. Truth was, she wouldn't mind talking about Petie. If there was an alpha male in a three-state radius, it was Tucker. After Mrs. Riddle's comments, Garnet really wouldn't mind hearing his opinion.

"A half hour," she conceded uneasily.

He smiled. A smile that knocked her common sense to its knees.

And then the boys descended on them, carrying a pan of water, most of which sloshed onto the floor, an ice pack, a brown bottle of betaine and a giant first-aid box. The principal and school secretary trailed right behind the boys.

Garnet closed her eyes and wished she could click her heels together three times and land in Kansas. How much worse could a bad day get?

Chapter Two

Apparently the day could get much, much worse—but Garnet couldn't guess that. Initially the drive home from school lifted her spirits.

On the third turn, she saw the sign for Plain Vanilla. A quarter mile later, blacktop turned to gravel, and the hot, brilliant sun disappeared, turned into the fragrant shade of pine forest. One more turn in the road, and her pride and joy came into view.

Petie scrabbled from the old van in a flash. Once he'd seen his report card—all As except for a C in gym—he never asked another thing about her meeting with Mrs. Riddle. School, schedules and the Mrs. Riddles in his life were now completely forgotten. All those academic As had earned him the right to download the latest game he wanted.

Garnet climbed from the van more slowly. Her right foot was still smarting, her head doing an annoying little throb—but she didn't really care. She took a long, lazy moment to cherish the view.

Her five acres had been scrap-scrub when she bought them six years before. No one thought she could make anything of it—especially not her parents, and heaven knew, she had a long, *long* history of disappointing her family.

Plain Vanilla had been the straw that broke the camel's back.

It had almost broken hers.

Four customers were parked below the shop—not bad, for midday on a Thursday. Nothing about Plain Vanilla was fancy. The building had shake-shingle siding, with a long overhang for a traditional country-style porch. Unless a serious storm threatened, the double screen doors were kept open and welcoming. Pots of herbs and flowers added color.

The parking lot was known to get a little weedy, but she could already inhale the scents emanating from the shop. Basil and chives. Lavender and vanilla. Scents hung low in this tuck of valley. So, of course, did the heat.

Her bungalow was invisible from here, behind the shop, but to the right stretched open ground—the hodgepodge of raised beds and climate-controlled greenhouses where she grew her own herbs and spices. Two years ago, she—and the bank—had added horizontal blinds that could be opened or closed, to protect the plants from too much sun.

Except for the fancy blinds, she'd made everything herself. There'd never been money for professionals... but she'd had two staff from the start, primarily because she couldn't work 24-hour days and handle Petie, especially when he'd been little.

And from inside the shop, she suddenly heard two women's voices…and suspected her son had tattled about her being hurt, because two bodies hightailed down the porch steps faster than she could run for cover.

Mary Lou was somewhere between fifty-five and ninety-five, tougher than beef jerky, and looked it. Her health was precarious, not that she'd admit it. Garnet had "discovered her" five years ago, when Mary Lou had shown up at the back door, fixed her with a scissor-sharp scowl, said her husband was dead, she was bored out of her skull, and she needed to work, no wages needed, just a *job.*

Garnet had hired her and never looked back. If a thief ever came around, Mary Lou would probably scare him to death, and heaven knew she was a worker.

"Garnet! Peter said you were hurt! Who did what to you, you tell me right now!"

"It was just a couple of bumps, absolutely nothing."

Mary Lou frowned, but then immediately went off on her own bumps that day. "Well, this morning was a blinger. First off, the postman forgot to leave me stamps and I was going to pay bills. Then Georgia Cunningham, she came in, bought fifty dollars' worth of all kinds of things, put two twenties on the counter and left. Just like that. I was going to call the police, but then I thought I'd wait until you got home. But I think she should spend the night in jail, myself. Ten dollars! She cheated us of ten dollars! I never…"

Then it was Sally, striding right behind her. "Peter said there was a man who knocked you down—"

"It was a complete accident. No biggie. What's wrong?"

Sally had dark caramel skin, hair done in dreads and a perpetual frown that did a great job of concealing a gorgeous face. She had two kids and a no-good husband. She worked like a fiend, loved the plants as much as Garnet did and could stand up for herself anywhere she needed to—except at home.

Garnet could tell when her jerk-water husband had done something because Sally's hands would start jittering; she couldn't stand still.

"I got a rash on the lavender."

"Which one?"

"The French blue. They're just speckles on the leaves, but they weren't there yesterday. I've been trying to look it up. We don't want it spreading. But you know me and reading those stupid manuals—"

"I know. It's okay. We'll go check it out."

And that was how it went, one crisis after another all afternoon. Early on, she hustled home to talk to Pete—and to make sure he'd had lunch. But of course, being Petie, he'd made himself a sandwich, cleaned up and naturally parked in front of his computer…a water-cooled system that he'd put together himself last Christmas.

She ruffled his mop of brown hair—hair so luxuriously thick she was jealous of it. He was scrunched up in his computer chair, imitating a human pretzel. "Hey. I didn't get a chance to tell you what Mrs. Riddle had to say."

"Not now, Mom. I'm at level four."

"Okay. We can talk about it later, I guess." She hesitated. "Mr. MacKinnon's coming over for a little while after dinner."

"You mean Will's dad? That Mr. MacKinnon?"

"Yes."

"Is Will coming over, too?"

"I don't know. He might."

"Okay. Whatever."

No "why" or "what for?" He didn't care. He pushed his glasses higher on his nose, then bent his head to the game again. She couldn't resist giving him a fast smooch on his forehead. Now that he was ten, she had to steal kisses, kidnap hugs.

"*Mom.* I'm creating an alternate universe right now. It's really hard."

"Okay, okay." She smiled…but the smile faded in seconds. This was exactly what Mrs. Riddle had implied. Petie was all too happy alone. Everything he loved had always been inside. He'd just never been the kind of kid to play outside, getting into scrapes and mud with playmates.

So, she told herself there was no reason to get nervous about Tucker stopping by. It was a good idea. Single parents had problems that two-parent families just didn't have. As different as their sons were, it'd be nice to talk to someone else who lived with a ten-year-old. It wasn't like a *personal* meeting. Or a date. Or anything remotely like that.

She couldn't imagine Tucker looking at her that way.

The women in her family were bred to be hothouse Southern belles, Charleston style, women who could do the debutante thing and have dinner for forty—with fresh flowers and crystal—prepared in an hour's notice. Garnet wasn't adopted, although when she was eleven, she'd checked to make sure. Something had gone wrong, anyway. Her sisters and mom—even her grandmother—had gracious beauty and poise without even trying.

She'd been born plain vanilla. Always had been, always would be.

The *point,* though, was that she never got back in the

house until nearly six. She'd wanted a shower and clean clothes and a major spiff-up before Tucker got there. Instead, life just kept interfering. Sally needed help with updating Plain Vanilla's website and Facebook page, which Garnet loved on a par with triple taxes and bee stings. And then Mary Lou cornered her in the back-room, where new herb and spice recipes needed a taste test and review.

By the time Garnet finally charged back home, Petie had made dinner—peanut butter and banana sand-wiches, one of his specialties, followed by fresh brown-ies. Brownies were one of Petie's favorite creations. This time he'd added raspberries, blueberries and marshmal-lows. She never knew what he was going to put in next.

"Hey, I'd have made you dinner," she told him.

"Yeah, well, you were busy and I was starving for peanut butter and banana sandwiches. Mom…"

"What?"

"You know that crazy-looking cat that's been around for the last week or so?"

"The black-and-orange-and-white one?"

"Yeah. I think she's pregnant, because I saw her on the window sill about an hour ago, and her stomach was, like, huge."

"No," Garnet said.

"I never asked you anything."

"You were going to."

Petie shot her a look, one of his most endearing. "I understand why you said no. You have to feel like you're the one in charge. We'll talk about it later."

She chased after him with a dish towel. "Sometimes you sound older than Methuselah."

"Just because I'm smarter than you?"

"Petie. We can't adopt every single animal who wanders on our porch!"

"Yes, Mom."

"I'm still recovering from the ferret you took in."

"Yes, Mom."

"And the raccoon babies."

"Yes, Mom." He said consolingly, "It's okay for you to say no. Really. I won't feel neglected or deprived or anything like that."

She couldn't shoot the kid. He was the best thing in her world. She loved him more than life. But he *was* getting a mouth, and their teasing took another twenty minutes off the clock. She charged into the bathroom, took one look in the mirror and knew she didn't remotely have enough time. She needed a shower, a hair wash, her foot rebandaged, a haircut, a hair style, a wardrobe refurbishing, shaved legs, time to buy some makeup in town, maybe some jewelry and new sandals.

She also needed to clean her bedroom—not because anyone was going to see it, but because so many things were strewn all over the place that she couldn't find anything.

A few minutes after seven, Petie yelled from the living room, "Hey, Mom, Mr. MacKinnon is here!"

Well, at least she'd progressed from being naked. The cream linen shirt was ancient, but it was softer than silk and had a band collar. It was her lucky shirt. Her feel-safe shirt. Her hair was still wet, but she'd made a makeshift fat braid, used a tortoiseshell comb to pin it off her head. The capris were clean. And that was the end of her grooming.

She'd have put sandals on, but they were by the back door. She'd put on lipstick, but hadn't gotten around to the dishes. She'd bandaged her foot, but the coffee table was still heaped with folded clothes that—yet again—refused to put themselves away.

When it came down to it, just showing up was the best she could manage.

Petie was doing a far better job of taking care of their guest. He was sprawled on top of the couch as if he was an afghan, lazily slinging a dirty bare foot in the air. He'd served their guest a sweating glass of grape Kool-Aid and opened a package of Oreos.

"My theory," Pete was explaining to Tucker, "is that when school's out, you should get to forget about it. You should get to do stuff you like. Summer should be about not worrying... Hey, Mom. Mr. MacKinnon's here."

"I see him. And I heard when you called me the first time. Welcome, Tucker."

He stood up, not the polite way a boarding-school kid learned to stand when a lady entered the room. It was more of a long, lanky stretching up. He went from a nice, reasonable-sized man sitting in a chair, to a six-three hunk of space that instantly stole all the oxygen in the room.

There was nothing manicured about Tucker. His eyebrows were the same scruffy brown as his hair...and the stubble on his chin. The shirt was clean, no more wrinkled than his cotton pants, and his slow smile looked as lazy as the rest of him. The blue eyes were sexy blue. Laser-riveting blue. Dizzy blue. Or maybe that was just how she reacted to him.

It certainly wasn't Tucker's fault he made her knees want to buckle. She should have matured years ago. She kept meaning to. As soon as she had time. For now, unfortunately, he was the only man in a blue moon who had inspired a completely ditzy, unreasonable, irrational crush.

"You've got quite a place here," he said easily.

"It's a work in progress. Would you like me to show you around?"

"Sure. That sounds good. Pete, you want to come with us?"

"Do I have to?" Pete asked her.

"Nope. Up to you."

She wished he'd come. She wanted a chaperone. Not to protect her from Tucker. To protect him from her. She was likely to make a damn fool of herself around him.

But showing him around the place gave her something to do, something to say. She started with the shop, because the bombardment of scents and textures usually pleased everybody—men as well as women.

"Wow. How'd you come up with all this?" he asked, almost the minute they walked in the door.

Naturally her pride swelled like a balloon. All this time, she'd never been able to talk to him, and now she couldn't stop. First, she explained how she'd arranged the shop, and why. Her herbs were all in pots, set in antique porcelain sinks, located so they'd get east light. The old porcelain added to the country-comfortable atmosphere, but also enabled her to set up a water-spraying system so the herbs could easily be misted.

Across the room, the west side held cubbyholes with books on medicinal and culinary uses for herbs and spices, with handwritten recipes that Garnet had started but her customers had added to. Color photographs identified what the herbs looked like in different seasons. The north wall had the least exposure to sunlight, so it was a natural spot to put counters and shelves for bottled or burlap-packed spices and herbs, with fresh samples displayed on small trenchers so a customer could smell and taste.

"Obviously the fresh samples aren't there now—we clean up at night. But lots of customers don't know the difference between cilantro and basil. That's why we have the samples and the books and the recipes…to give them ideas about how to use them."

"So what's back here?" Tucker motioned to a wooden half door leading to a space in the back.

She unhooked the gate to the half door and motioned him through so he could see. "We have classes back here… Sometimes we'll cater a lunch for a small group, or we'll use recipes to show folks how to use their herbs. This is also where we pot and arrange the plants. And there's one more room in the far back…."

She led the way ahead of him. The back room was her favorite, possibly because of its spectacularly wonderful messes. A board-plank table functioned as a work area, but every inch of space was used. Herbs dried from the ceiling and cubbyholes held rolls of ribbon and linen bags and string, while potting soil and tools and pots took up another heap of space. "And this is one of my serious treasures." She motioned to the climate-controlled aquarium that took up one complete wall. "I created this for a teaching tool. It's just a miniature woods to show some of the endangered species in our area. Like this plant, Gray's Lily…and the Glade Splurge here…and this is Mountain Bittercress…."

Her voice trailed off. She completely lost her train of thought. She glanced up and found him watching her. Until that instant she hadn't realized how close he was, how tall he was, and damn, if he didn't have the most wicked eyes. Alarm thrummed in her pulse. It was one thing to admit she had a crush, another to fool herself into believing he was looking at her with interest. *That* kind of interest.

She covered the awkward moment with a sudden quick laugh. "Well, I've been talking your ear off, haven't I? You didn't come here to hear about all this."

"Only because I didn't know what all you were doing here. I knew about the shop. Everybody does. But I didn't know you did all this interactive stuff with your customers. I mean, all the hands-on learning, side education, the whole shebang."

Garnet could feel a flush climb her neck, embarrassing the devil out of her. She just rarely heard praise.

"Well, isn't that similar to what you do?" she asked swiftly. "I know, you don't have a shop. But you have some kind of private school…?"

"Not a school. A camp and retreat center. I sort of fell into it. Had to do something with my mountain… I mean, there's some real beauty up top, a small lake, waterfalls, creeks, rocks, woods. It's too damned special not to share. So I take in groups. Boys in trouble. Companies having trouble with employees getting along. People wanting to start a new venture, make sure the whole new staff can cleave together."

"And then…?" She ambled back outside with him, exiting from the shop's back door. A slatted roof covered the breezeway to her bungalow, which provided shade but no mercy from the heat. Tonight, though, the oppressive temperatures had finally eased. A pale haze was stealing across the sky, softening the bright edges of the day.

"Well, what I do after that depends on the group," Tucker said. "I tend to start them out with some exercise—not work exercise, something fun. That gives me a baseline to work with. I get a picture of what the group can do—what the group might want to achieve together. I don't teach. I wouldn't know how to teach. But it's a little like what you created here. I try to expose people to things they haven't seen and done before. Hope to challenge them, to engage their natural interests. When something works, I build on that. Garnet...?"

She'd been listening, but when he said her name in a question, she lifted her head.

"I'd like to see everything you've got going outside, but maybe another time? I can see you're favoring that right foot. How about if we find a place to park for a few minutes?"

She wasn't going to deny her sore foot again. "You have no idea how well the limp's been working for me. I've been playing it up all day, making everyone else do the work, while I do the lazy Queen of Sheba routine."

He grinned. "Somehow I believe that, like I believe in the tooth fairy."

He had an odd way of making her feel comfortable... when she'd never imagined being comfortable around Tucker. He gravitated toward her front porch, where he probably spotted the old Adirondack rockers nested in the shade. It was a favorite spot for her. She couldn't see the road or the shop; she just had her private view of the mountain...and the acres she'd cultivated with greenhouses and raised gardens.

Tucker took it all in, as if the view were sipping whiskey. "Wow. You've got a lot to do here. Major work."

"It's taken a long time to get it this far. But I love it," she admitted.

"Is that a padlock I see on the far greenhouse?"

"Yes...it's pretty much the only thing I keep locked around here."

"For a special reason?"

"Oh, yeah. My vanilla plants are in there. It's the specialty of the whole place...not that I'm doing anything so brilliant. But it's a strain of vanilla I developed, so I need to guard it."

He'd cocked up a leg, started a slow, lazy rock. "Speaking of stuff that smells beyond irresistible—like vanilla—what's the thing I'm smelling around the porch?"

She motioned to the pots around the doors and steps. "Mint. It takes over if you just let it grow, but in pots it's easy enough to contain. They're not such pretty plants, but according to folklore, flying bugs and insects just don't like the smell, so they stay away."

For a second—just a small, small second—a silence fell. Because she'd never had the brains God gave a goose, she suddenly thought of a local folklore legend. Old-timers claimed that Whisper Mountain got its name from a "whispering wind" that only lovers heard.

In that small, small second of silence…she heard it. The whisper. The silken-soft whisper in the air. The achy sweet hum of yearning.

How stupid could she be? Annoyed with herself, she stabbed the porch floor with a heel and set her rocker at a creaky pace.

Tucker broke that dangerous silence. "How bad's the head?"

The bump on her head wasn't a problem. The brain inside her head was the problem, particularly if it was going to continue to respond to him like mush. "Our sons," she said, and thankfully the words functioned like a trigger to remind him why he'd stopped over.

"Yeah, I figured we'd better get into that." Tucker sighed, scratched an ear, made a comical face. "Mrs. Riddle scares the devil out of me, has from the first day of school. She makes me feel like I'll end up standing in the hall for some unknown wrongdoing. Anyway, she had a problem with my Will. Said for the last few months, he's become painfully shy around girls. Really miserable. Sweating, stumbling, can't talk."

She had to smile. "Don't you think all kids go through that?"

"Yeah, I do. But Will hit a massive growth spurt this year, shot up four inches, and I expect the mountain of hormones hit him before I was ready."

Out of nowhere, a cat showed up at the corner of the porch. Garnet instantly recognized it as the feline Pete had mentioned, because it was a she. A very, very pregnant she. There was some invisible sign on her property that invited only the critters who were pregnant and hungry. The cat was the color of mud, with a little Georgia red dirt thrown in, and eyes as gold as topaz. She started washing a paw, as if it was her porch and she'd always washed a paw there.

"Your cat?" Tucker asked.

"Absolutely not," she said firmly.

As if the cat sensed she was the subject of discussion, she twitched her tail and ambled over to Tucker's side. She hesitated for all of a millisecond, and then leaped on his lap.

"You're sure it's not yours?"

"Trust me. That cat will never be mine."

"Hmm. She doesn't seem wild."

He probably got that impression because the ornery, hardscrabble cat sleepily closed her eyes and started purring loud enough to wake the dead. Tucker shot her an amused look. He also gave the cat a long, soft stroke under her chin.

"Do *not* laugh at me. I'm learning to say no to Pete. It just doesn't happen to be a skill I'm particularly good at. But we simply *have* to stop adopting strays."

"Uh-huh. So how long do you think before she makes it into the house?"

All right. He made her laugh. "A week. At least I hope I can hold out that long." And then, because she was starting to feel comfortable with him in spite of herself, she asked carefully, "I don't know your circumstances, Tucker. I mean, I know you're a single parent like I am. But as far as Will's being extra nervous around girls...is there no mom in his picture?"

"There is. But she isn't what you'd call a helpful female influence on Will." Tucker sighed. "Angie's her name. We married before we finished college. My parents, her parents, everyone thought we were the perfect pair. For damn sure, she was the prettiest girl to ever graduate from Ole Miss, and back when I was twenty-one, I thought that was all that mattered. We've been divorced for around five years now. She got physical custody from the beginning, but Will never actually lived with her."

She frowned. "How'd that happen?"

"I know. It doesn't make a lot of sense. Angie decorates rich folks' houses in Atlanta. She's great at it. She claims she's putting all the child support money I send into a college fund for Will. I don't know if that's true or not. I just know that Will's happy with me, and there's no trouble as long as I keep sending the full quota of child support."

The picture Garnet formed of his ex-wife wasn't pretty...not that it was any of her business. "Will knows this? That she actually has physical custody even though he really stays with you?"

"Not exactly. I don't like lying to a kid, any kid...but I can't see telling Will something that would only hurt him, and for no possible purpose. She schedules four weekends or so a year to see him. And some holidays. She loves him. But...well, I think she was in a hustle to get married and have kids, but once the ring went on her finger and we had a kid, she was like a snail without a shell. The new role didn't fit. She never grew out of wanting to be a full-time Southern belle."

Garnet mulled how much he'd revealed of his life, and how easily. But he was already talking again.

"I didn't want to bore you to death with all that background. But I figured you might need to know... if you're inclined to go along with my plan."

"A plan?" she echoed.

The mottled cat leaped to the ground, washed another paw and then, as if she'd been asked, leaped up on Garnet's lap. Garnet firmly ignored her.

"I didn't hear all of what Mrs. Riddle had to say about your Pete. But I heard some. And I got this idea... that we could try trading kids, a few afternoons a week."

"Say what? Trade *kids?!*"

Chapter Three

Tucker had to grin. She looked pretty startled at the idea of swapping kids. At least he'd gotten her attention.

For *darn* sure, she'd gotten his. The business she'd set up was amazing. The shop, the grounds, the house. He'd never thought of her as a lightweight, but what she'd created here was downright remarkable.

And so was she.

"I didn't mean *literally* trade kids. But I got this brainstorm of how we could help each other. Starting with my Will... Just looking around here, I can see you've got plenty of manual work. He loves messing with dirt. And he's too young to have a 'real' job, but maybe you could find something helpful for him to do a couple afternoons a week?"

She didn't immediately answer, but he could almost hear the wheels turning in her mind as she considered the idea. She had to be concentrating mighty hard, because her right hand was instinctively stroking the cat on her lap—the cat she'd claimed wasn't hers and never would be. Finally, she came through with a worry. "Tucker, I'm not sure I'm the kind of feminine influence Mrs. Riddle thinks your Will needs."

"Are you kidding? You're perfect." He leaned forward, serious now, just struggling to find the right words to explain. "You're not froufrou. You're common sense. You clearly don't mind hard work. You're creative and interesting and smart, but not threatening. I think Will just being around you would help smooth out some of his current rough edges. Give him some confidence that all women aren't like his mom. That everyone without that Y chromosome isn't petrifying."

Hell. He'd said something wrong, but he wasn't sure what. The warm glow in her eyes turned abruptly cool. She stopped rocking. "Well, in some ways you're certainly right," she said swiftly. "I'm not remotely a froufrou kind of woman. Much less the kind of girl who'd fit into a sorority at Ole Miss."

That was the thorn? He thought he was giving her a major compliment. But he never had a chance to respond, because she took the conversational ball. "I'd be happy to have Will around here…but what if he doesn't want to? Maybe he won't like me, or the things I'm doing here."

"Well, I put a question to him at dinner. I've always had a heavy work schedule in the summer, and he's always spent those summers with me. We have a good time. But I just asked him if he'd like a change, like a chance to spend a few afternoons a week somewhere else. Do something different, learn something different. Help someone out. I didn't put your name out there,

I just put out the general idea. And he leaped on it. I think he'd really like it."

Before she could say no—and Tucker could smell when a woman was about to tell him no…God knew, he'd heard it enough—he added, "And I've got a plan for your Pete. And for you."

There. Mention her kid, and her face lit up with warmth again. Tucker tried to remember the last time he'd been this captivated by a woman…and couldn't. Talking to her only snared his attention more. For darn sure, he couldn't stop looking at her.

She was wearing a sort-of-white linen shirt, not sheer, but still light as sunlight, a soft caress of a drape on her shoulders, her breasts, a long, low V-neck revealing a delicate expanse of neck. She wore a tiny gold chain. Nothing glitzy or blingy, nothing like formal jewelry. The chain was just the thinnest collar of gold that glinted when she moved, drew attention to her sun-kissed skin beneath.

And then there were legs. For a pipsqueak, she had amazing legs. Slim calves, shapely thighs… Hell. Her knees were even cute.

Naturally he was attracted to her boobs and fanny— he was a guy. But her mouth revved his testosterone switch, too. Her lips looked vulnerable, bare, softer than satin. Maybe her mouth was a little wide, but that just made her smiles and laughter bigger, showed off those pretty teeth. It was a kissable mouth. Probably, on a scale of one to ten, it rated a fifteen-plus for kissability.

Not that he still played those immature scale games.

It was just…he hadn't let a woman close enough to *think* of those old immature scale games…in a blue moon.

"About my Petie…"

He straightened up. "Yeah. Here's my thought on Pete. I didn't mean to eavesdrop, but I heard part of what Mrs. Riddle said to you. She thinks Pete needs a sport, something outside of academics—"

"It's not that he doesn't get along with the other kids," Garnet interrupted, immediately defending her son. "She was just making a point that middle school is tough on all kids. And she thought he'd fit in better with the boys…if he had some kind of athletic skill."

Tucker nodded, then wedged a little closer. "I heard from somebody—probably another parent—that you were a widow?"

Her voice picked up a careful cadence, making him pretty sure—damned sure—she was giving him the spruced-up version of the story. "Yes, that's right. Johnny and I ran off, got married right out of high school. It's no secret I was pregnant at the time. He thought the best way to earn a living was to go into the service. Unfortunately, only a few months later he was sent to the Middle East. He came home on every leave, it's not as if we never saw him, but he died when Pete was barely three. He just wasn't around to be a male influence."

"I take it there's no other family close? Your parents? His grandparents from the other side?"

"John's family moved to Oregon years ago. They send presents, cards, but otherwise haven't tried to be part of Petie's life. And my family's originally from Charleston. Two sisters. No brothers."

When she didn't add anything further about her family, he thought, *ho-kay.* Obviously there was a sore spot…which made Tucker conclude that she'd never had much backup coming from family.

"So," he said slowly, "I don't care what Mrs. Riddle

said. What do you think? About whether Pete needs a sport, or to develop some kind of athletic skill, or just some guy time?"

She tucked a strand of hair behind her ear. "I don't see why every boy should be inherently great with sports…any more than every girl plays with dolls. Pete's smart as a whip. He can cook better than I can. He built his own computer. Sometimes he'll come out and work with me, so it's not like he's afraid to get his hands dirty. He just seems to like being inside more."

"What sports have you tried?"

"Well…swimming. Hiking. I know, that doesn't sound like much…but it hasn't been that easy. I'm really tied down with Plain Vanilla. I have two regular employees, but that's it. On Sundays, especially during the school year, we often take off and do something. It's just…Petie would rather do a movie or prowl around a computer store. Sports never seem to make it on his want-to-do list."

Tucker nodded. "That's kind of what I thought you'd say. So here's my plan. Let me take your Pete, while you have my Will. Same setup. Trade kids a couple afternoons a week. Pete can just hang with me… I've got a range of groups coming in over the next few weeks. It'll be easy to give him a chance to try new things. At his size, I'm guessing you're not real hot on the idea of contact sports, so we'll concentrate on the other kind. Kayaking, archery, rock climbing. Not that he *has* to try anything. He'll just get the chance. No push. No bribery. Just see if he shows an interest, and if he does, I'll work with him on it. I mean…if he goes along with the idea."

"That sounds good," she said slowly. "Better than good. I'd really like to give it a try—if our boys are for it."

A silence fell. At least for Tucker, it felt like an elephant suddenly plunked down on her front porch. They'd been talking easily, naturally, but once the topic of their sons was over, Garnet stiffened up.

"Well," he said, "I should be getting back."

She vaulted from the chair as if spring-loaded. "Me, too. I still have things I have to do tonight."

He got it. She wanted him to leave. And hell. He *did* need to get back to his place. But standing next to each other, he felt like a bear next to delicate crystal. He said slowly, "It bugged me all day. That you were hurt because of me this morning."

"That's silly, Tucker. It was a complete accident. No harm done."

Yeah, he'd heard all that before.

"Yeah? Well, I've watched you a couple times reach for the back of your head. How big's the goose egg?"

"It's nothing," she said for what seemed like the zillionth time, but he was all through buying that malarkey.

He was already within touching distance. One step closer, and he could ease a palm around her neck and gently push her head into his chest. She didn't fight him as he felt for the scar. In fact, she seemed to quit breathing altogether. The texture of her silky hair, tangling around his fingers, tangoed with the fresh smell of her shampoo and caused the obvious physical reaction in him. He ignored the arousal. He wanted to see the cut, for Pete's sake.

And he found it. It wasn't actually a goose egg, but looked more like a burn mark. Buried in her hair, but looking raw and fiery. "Ouch," he said. "What's wrong with you, that you haven't been whining and yelling? Take advantage. Heave on some guilt."

He stepped back, so she'd quit worrying he was going to jump her. He wanted to. Really, really wanted to. But obviously he was going to have to earn her trust by baby steps. A zillion of them. And when he stepped back, he won a reluctant grin...possibly because she liked his joking tone.

"I admit, it still smarts."

"I'll bet it does. So I owe you. You just have to think about what and when you want to collect." He was using his best teasing tone, but abruptly realized that his fingers were still in her hair, drifting through that soft, silky sea, no longer looking for hurts and scrapes, just... feeling.

He dropped his hand, but all that provocative *feeling* was still there. Electrified because she was looking at him. Because their eyes met and neither could seem to break the sudden sharp connection between them. He could smell that raspberry shampoo of hers. See the pulse in the hollow of her throat. Hear the worry and tension in her scattered breath.

He'd known it'd be like this. Or he'd hoped it would. All he'd wanted was the chance to spend some time with her, be with her, do something to make her notice. Not notice *him*. But notice that something had a chance of firing hot and bright between them.

But he figured, for now, he'd pushed enough. He smiled, made a slow, easy business out of fishing the truck keys from his side pocket, letting her see that he was leaving. A little worry was fine. A few nerves were fine. But she really did seem like a fawn, standing in bright headlights, ready to bolt and flee.

He had no idea what made her so wary, but now, he just might have a chance to find out.

"How about trying the plan with the boys, say, next Tuesday afternoon?"

"Sure. That sounds fine." But her eyes hadn't left his. Her voice still couldn't muster more power than a whisper.

"I think we've got a good idea. If it doesn't work, then it doesn't. But no harm in giving it a try."

"I agree. I appreciate your coming up with the plan."

He shot her an easy smile, took one step off her porch. "You know the old legend about Whisper Mountain, don't you?"

She started to speak, then seemed to correct herself. "I heard a really foolish story, about when the wind's coming from a certain direction, people can hear the sound of voices, or something like that."

She wasn't getting off that easy. "The legend is that it's a lovers' wind. That only lovers can hear the mountain whisper."

"Silliest thing I ever heard," she said.

"Yeah. That's what I think, too," he concurred, and with another grin, strode off toward his truck...just as the sky opened with a noisy crack of thunder.

Well, *fine,* Garnet thought irritably, as she yanked on a yellow slicker and fumbled in the back hall for a flashlight. Hard to imagine this day getting any more upsetting. First there'd been the stomach-knotting talk with Mrs. Riddle, then the foot and head scrapes that hurt the whole darned afternoon, then behaving like a goose with Tucker...and no, of course she had no illusions what'd been going on there. He'd been kind. Looking at her sore head.

She was the one imagining his interest...when she knew perfectly well she was invisible to men. Always had been. Always would be. Particularly with power-house alpha guys like Tucker.

And now, an unexpected torrential rain put a sharp cap on the day. "Petie!" she called from the back door. "I'm going to check on the greenhouses!"

She heard a distant "okay," then pelted outside into the deluge. The rain was warm, coming down in sheets, making the ground slick and blurring her vision. Her plants—all of them—loved rain more than well water, but a downpour like this could erode the soil and smash down delicate leaves.

She unlocked the door to her precious vanilla house first, then checked the other greenhouses at a run, ending up at the raised garden beds closest to the shop. The raised beds all had "shade curtains"—mesh that rolled out twelve feet above ground. The curtain protected the plants from too much sun as well as allowing rain in—but not this kind of gully-washing rain. She cranked out the roll of curtain, which shouldn't have been hard...except that her hands were wet and her eyes blinded with rain.

The whole task shouldn't have taken fifteen minutes, but by the time she charged back into the house, she was soaked to the bone and trailing more water than a river. "I'm back!" she called, so Petie wouldn't worry.

She peeled off the slicker and shoes, exchanged the rest of her clothes in the bedroom for a long robe, grabbed a brush and started tracking down her son.

Likely he'd be near either a TV or computer screen, but that hardly limited the possibilities. Her bungalow was built in the old-fashioned Southern style, with all rooms having a window view, and storage located in the windowless center of the place. The back side—the woods and mountain sides—had her bedroom, a den/ TV room and Pete's bedroom, which she checked first.

His sanctuary had walls of cracked pine, with a built-in desk and shelves. Unlike her bedroom, Pete's bed was tidily made and his clothes put away. The only noise in the room came from a pair of hamsters, furiously running their wheels. She spotted Pete's bare feet propped on the bed, but she had to lean over the bed to find the rest of her son. Petie was nestled in a down comforter on the floor, reading from a Kindle.

"Well, if this isn't petrifying," she said. "Is the sky falling? Your laptop's shut down. The TV's off."

"Mom. There was some thunder. I had to turn everything off." Behind glasses too dirty to see, Petie's eyes looked hopelessly mournful.

"But it looks like you found a book to read." She perched on the bed, resisted the urge to tickle his feet.

"Actually, it's boring. And how come Mr. MacKinnon came over, anyway?"

She was ready for the question. "We were trying to think up a plan to torture you and his Will."

"If you can't think up a better story than that, I'm going back to my book."

"I'm serious! We came up with the idea that you and Will might like to trade places for a couple afternoons."

Pete marked the spot in his Kindle and shut down. *Now* his eyes were suspicious. "Why would we want to do that?"

"Because summer vacations are fun. But they can also be boring."

He crossed his skinny arms. "Mom, I'm about never bored. You *know* that."

"I do. But Mr. MacKinnon has a gorgeous spot on top of the mountain. There's a lake up there. Cliffs—"

"I know. We had a field trip there a couple years ago. It's pretty awesome."

"That's what I thought—"

Pete interrupted her. "Just tell me straight. Is this one of your schemes to make me 'go outside and have fun'?"

She tried to think of a way to color up the truth. Couldn't think of any. "Sort of," she had to admit.

Petie emitted one of his old-soul's sighs. "Listen. You need me. If I'm not here, you can't find your car keys. And you put the milk in the cupboard. And sometimes you forget it's dinnertime. And sometimes you need me to help with the plants and stuff."

"That's all true. I do need you. And you're wonderful at being responsible and taking care of things," Garnet agreed. "But that's not a lot of fun for you."

"Mom. I don't know why you can't get it. I have fun all the time. It's just not *noisy* fun." He sighed again. "This is about something Mrs. Riddle said to you, isn't it? She says I never cause trouble. She says it's not natural. So she got you all worried that you're not a great mother, right?"

It scared her. If he could out-think her at age ten, how could she possibly cope when he was a teenager? "Not exactly."

"Okay. We'll go through this again. You're a great mom. Even if you forget and put the peanut butter in the fridge. Even if you dance around like a goon when you're making cookies. But this is like when Grandma and Grandpa call. You get all upset. You start scrubbing floors. You gotta quit listening to other people. Listen to me."

"Peter. Sometimes you need to remember that I'm the parent, and you're the kid. Sometimes I actually know a little more about life than you do."

"When?"

"Hey. That wasn't funny. It was mean."

He rolled his eyes to the ceiling. "Okay, okay. I'll go over to Mr. MacKinnon's if you want me to. It's not like it's terrible there. He's a good guy and all." His tone conveyed that he was caving, but she'd better realize she was going to owe him forever for agreeing to this.

"I just want you to try it a couple of times. See if you like the setup there. That's all I'm asking. For you to check it out."

"Okay, okay. I said I would."

She escaped while she was ahead, aimed for the kitchen and the end-of-the-day cleanup. There wasn't much. Crumbs here, a quick sweep, a couple glasses to pop in the dishwasher, and last, scouring the sink. Garnet knew perfectly well she was the worst housekeeper in the universe, so heaven knew how she'd picked up an obsession about a clean sink, but there it was. Another character flaw.

By the time the sink had a blinding gleam, her mind had skidded back to Tucker. How she felt around him. How she didn't want to feel. How every single thing that happened today had been...unsettling.

MacKinnons were blue blood in this part of the country. So was *her* family...but not her. She was plain vanilla all the way, went to bed with the first boy who asked her, got instantly pregnant, married Johnny because she was wildly in love with him—but he chose to fight in the Middle East rather than live with her. She wasn't just an underachiever in her family.

She was the one who always made the wrong choices.

Tucker, with his background, had understandably been attracted to—and married—a sorority girl from Ole Miss. So the marriage hadn't worked out. Eventually he'd find another woman with the beauty and grace and class of a traditional Southern belle, because that's what MacKinnons did.

And Garnet would still be working in the dirt, struggling to make an ordinary living, to just raise her son and do a good job at it.

Nothing wrong with that.

But she'd made enough bad judgments. Her heart was impulsive and unpredictable. Her life had gone much, much easier since she'd just kind of abandoned men. And that resolve hadn't changed just because she had a major zing thing for Tucker.

She'd had zings before. They always turned out wrong.

A razor-sharp blade of lightning knifed the sky, followed by an angry growl of thunder...as if she needed a reminder that she and nature didn't always get along.

Chapter Four

Tucker glanced at his watch. What was it about Tuesdays? He'd been chasing his tail all morning, and now it was almost 1:00 p.m. "Hey, Will! Get the lead out!" he yelled, as he hiked toward the truck.

A group of fifty high-school kids were scheduled around five, and before they arrived, there was still a ton of prep to do. The camp cook needed a sort-out of the menu. The truck bringing supplies and freezer goods for the week was overdue. The camp counselors needed one last run-through of the week's activity plans before the new gang arrived.

He'd volunteered to drop Will at Plain Vanilla—and pick up Pete at the same time. But running this late, he just needed to get the show on the road.

Will lumbered outside, shot his father a look, then lumbered into the truck. Tucker recognized his son's "delinquent" face. As soon as they were buckled in, he turned the key. "What's the silent deal? I thought you were on board with this idea."

"I was. Until I got a stomachache."

"When did the stomachache hit?"

"About an hour ago."

About an hour ago—if Tucker remembered right—Will had taken off right after an early lunch with a fly rod. He'd come back whistling, changed clothes. Now, the silence.

Only one road led down from the mountaintop. One corkscrew turn followed another. Each bend and twist showed a different vista—a flash of mountain cliff, the velvet of green wooded shade, a burst of sunlight. Tucker had driven the road a million times, never tired of it. He wouldn't use the word *magical* because that was too corny. But he'd never been able to put an anxious childhood behind him until settling on the mountain for good.

Growing up a MacKinnon had made Tucker determined that Will's childhood would be different than his.

"Did you change your mind about working with Garnet?" he asked his son.

"No. Not exactly."

"But you're bugged about something."

"Not exactly."

"Could you maybe pin down some 'exactlys' for me?"

Will scowled. "Her place is kind of interesting. She's okay, too. I mean, she was at school a lot. So I know she's okay."

"But…?" Sometimes communicating with his son was like trying to prod a bear out of hibernation.

"But she might not want me around, Dad. I don't want her to be stuck with me."

Because Tucker didn't have a temper, he didn't want to wring his ex-wife's neck. He just calmly, rationally considered how much damn harm the woman had done to their son. "Garnet *asked* if you were willing to help her. She's not even as tall as you, Will. Probably doesn't weigh nearly as much. And there are no guys around there. She was just hoping you might be willing to do some guy-type projects with her."

"I told you. I like that idea. In fact, I was really charged to go this morning. I don't even care if she pays me. It's just…"

Tucker waited. Waiting had always been fun for him. Like poking a needle at a toothache.

"…I just don't know if I'll know what to say to her."

His son was worried about *that?* Hell, Tucker didn't have a clue what to say to her, either. It'd taken several years of their sons being in the same class for Garnet to even recognize he was alive. And then he'd practically had to knock her down to win some conversation.

Less than ten minutes passed before they pulled into her drive. A half-dozen cars were parked in front of the shop, a variety of customers wandering around outside. Still, he noticed her first.

Her hair was bunched under a straw hat. She was wearing a sleeveless tank with the Plain Vanilla logo, shorts, sandals. She was laughing with a customer. The sun sheened on her bare shoulders and toned upper arms.

She shaded her forehead when she saw the truck, left the customer and immediately strode toward them with a smile. A smile, Tucker noted, that was for Will rather than him.

"Hey, guys." She had a no-nonsense stride, pure girl, but still lithe and easy. "Man, am I glad you're here,

Will. I have a problem you could really help me with. It's a secret that I just can't share with anyone here. So I need somebody I can trust."

"I can keep a secret," Will promised her.

"Great. You don't mind getting a little dirty, do you?"

"No. It's okay. I like getting dirty."

"No kidding?" Garnet shot Tucker a quick wink, but really, she hadn't noticed him yet. She was still all about straight eye contact with Will. "I figured by midafternoon, we'd both need a break. But I wasn't sure what you liked to snack on? So I got a couple different kinds of juice, made some fresh chocolate chip cookies..."

"I *really* like cookies."

"Oh, thank heavens. I wasn't sure." She shot Tucker another wink, but unless he stood on his head, he doubted she was ever going to look at him directly.

The screen door to the store banged open, and out came Pete. Tucker wanted to scratch his neck. Petie had the same expression as his Will had had this morning. The Christian-entering-the-Romans'-lion's-den look. The long-suffering look. The I'll-do-this-but-you'll-have-to-kill-me-to-have-fun look.

"Hey, Pete," Tucker said.

"Hey, Mr. MacKinnon." The kid was dressed appropriately. Sturdy shorts. Short-sleeved shirt. Running shoes. His hair looked like a cap, as if it'd been cut with a bowl, and framed his face, showed off his round glasses...and the half-dozen freckles on his nose.

"I'm glad we're trying this trade thing," Tucker said genially. "Your mom said you're pretty good with numbers, organizing things."

"Yeah. I am, sometimes."

"I'm not sure anyone can organize me, Pete. Grown

men have tried. But I sure could use some help if you'd be willing to give it a shot."

The face looked a little brighter. Still five shades of glum, but not quite so miserable.

"Well, hop in and we'll take off."

Petie did…and for all of three and a half seconds, Tucker had Garnet's attention. She came closer to the truck door, took off the straw hat. Her hair shivered and shook in the sun, finally freed from confinement, making him think that's how it'd look when she woke up in the morning. Or after a nap.

Or right after making love.

That thought came from nowhere. Tucker punched his inner censor, smiled at her like a normal human being instead of the lovesick idiot he was turning into around her. "Not sure of this…" he murmured.

"You, too? I'm afraid we've invited a disaster on each other."

"Yeah. I saw the expressions. Well…we'll retrade around six-thirty?"

"Sounds right. I'll bring Will earlier if there's any problem or he wants to go home." She lifted a hand.

He got it, she wanted to touch knuckles. They were, after all, in this project together. So he leaned forward to touch her knuckles, and again, she looked straight at him.

Just like that, it happened again. A wildfire of emotion, torching through his veins. Need, coiling like a snake. Want, whispering like silk through his witless mind.

His response was adolescent and annoying as hell.

But it was real.

If their sons would just go along with their crazy plan, he'd have chances to see her again. To be around her. To see if she ever peeled off that careful, friendly veneer for a man…or if she could be coaxed to.

Garnet was late—not for the first time—but there was no speeding on the twisty curves near the mountaintop. She breathed a sigh of relief when she finally saw the hand-carved sign reading MacKinnon Breakaway.

Next to her, Will immediately piped up, "Yeah, that's us. The house is on the right, Mrs. G."

She pulled into the driveway and braked. The plan was to drop off Will and pick up Petie—and immediately skedaddle. Her son had to be starving. She sure was.

Still, she soaked in the view for a few moments. She had to admit she'd been curious about where Tucker lived.

"The house started out as my great-grandpa's," Will told her. "But my grandpa just called it the lodge. But when we moved here, my dad built cabins for all the campers and retreaters to stay. He didn't want strangers underfoot right where he lived. That's what he said, anyway."

"It's really cool," she told him.

"Yeah, I know." Will opened the van door and hit the ground running. She followed more slowly, still studying the sprawling log home. It wasn't really as big as a lodge, more set up as a country place that could accommodate a big family or family gatherings. Gabled roof. Two stone chimneys. Old, majestic shade trees. A veranda on the second story, wrapping around the whole house.

Garnet could easily picture waking up in the morning, sliding open the door and stepping onto that veranda, seeing for miles from that mesmerizing mountaintop.

"Hello there!" The front door suddenly opened, and a barefoot woman stepped out. "You must be Garnet. Will ran through here faster than lightning."

"Yes. I'm Garnet." She smiled a greeting, but on the inside, she was kicking herself from here to Poughkeepsie. Of course Tucker had a woman in his life. How could a virile guy like him not? She wasn't surprised. At all. In any way.

Not even a little.

The woman was tall and lean, wearing shorts and a T-shirt, but also one of those "serious" safari vests with a zillion pockets. Her hair was cropped short, pale blond like cornstalks, fair skin with a light coating of tan and freckles, eyes a gorgeous blue. Garnet guessed she was several years younger than Tucker.

"Come on in. Tucker just paged that he and your son were still in the office, but they were locking up. I'm guessing they'll be here in less than five. It's a short hike." The blonde reached out a friendly hand, looking her over as intently as Garnet had her. "I'm Rosemary. Want me to see if I can scare up some iced tea?"

"Thanks, but no need to. As soon as I pick up Pete, we need to head home."

From nowhere, Rosemary suddenly laughed. "I'm just his sister, Garnet. There are three of us. Tucker's the oldest, then Ike, and then came me, the family surprise. Anyway, I got a summons from Tucker. When anything goes wrong in the family, Tucker's our frontline fixer, and the family's determined I need fixing."

That was a lot to share with a stranger, but Garnet appreciated the candid spill. "You don't look like you need fixing."

"Try telling my brothers that, would you? And the parents. They all think I've turned into a hermit." She ushered Garnet up the porch steps, into the cooler shade, still talking. "I'm a botanist. Got a fabulous grant to study the wild orchids in South Carolina."

"Wow. That sounds fascinating. I have a place— Plain Vanilla—where I'm growing herbs and spices. I try to concentrate on plants that grow naturally in this area. Except for vanilla, of course, but most people don't realize that vanilla—"

"Is really an orchid. Oh, my. We're going to get along really well. I hope Tucker doesn't show up for eons—"

But he did, right then, pulling up in a dirt-crusted Gator. He tripped the key, jumped out, and just that fast, the yard was electrified by two hundred pounds of male, virile energy. Tucker met her eyes before she could duck. And there it was, that sipping-slow smile of his, that went to her head faster than Southern bourbon.

"It's not my fault we're late," he said immediately.

"Yeah, Mom, it was all mine." Petie leaped from the Gator and barreled toward her. "Do we have to go *now?* I don't want to leave yet."

Confusion reigned for several minutes. Rosemary claimed a hug from her big brother and started a mutually insulting sibling banter, then Will suddenly hurtled out the screen doors onto the porch, came right up to her, his face more flushed than beets, and said, "Hey. I shoulda said thank you. I forgot. I hope it's okay if I come back."

"Of course it's okay. You were a terrific help," Garnet assured him. Next to her, Petie tried to engage Tucker in some sort of technical business regarding the camp website. They might as well have been talking Swahili, for all Garnet understood.

Tucker seemed to manage the multiple conversations just fine...until he suddenly put up a hand in a signal for silence. "Hey. Everyone chill for a couple minutes. Just a couple minutes. I'd really like to take Garnet to the Tower. We'll make it the quickest trip on record. But she told me she really wanted to see it."

She'd never said any such thing, but when she turned around to send him an astonished look, he was already propelling her down the porch steps with a hand at her back. He motioned toward the Gator. "That's the chariot I use to get around the camp. Hop in."

She did. It only took a quick minute to realize that he'd wrangled this time alone so they could pass notes on how their kids responded to the afternoon.

"You first. How'd it work out with Will?" he asked.

They were already a distance from the house, and after a sharp curve, she saw the sign for the Breakaway office. Where Petie had hung out that afternoon? She wanted to ask, but then he glanced at her...with one of *those* looks.

She'd never had a chance to change before bringing Will home, which meant she was still wearing old Tevas, a paisley tie for her hair, the usual Plain Vanilla shirt and shorts...and some extra decoration in the form of smudges and dirt. The way he gave her an up-and-down suggested she looked fine. Beyond fine.

The man needed glasses or medication for dementia...but he quit with the monkey business, once she answered his question about Will.

"You told me Will was ultra shy with women? Tucker—he talked my ear off. I know more about your family than you probably wanted me to hear. I know about the girl he likes. What he thinks of his mother. How he doesn't see much of his grandma and grandpa, but your sister and brother are regulars in his life. He told me heaps of things that are none of my business, but I swear, I didn't ask him—and would never have asked him—personal questions."

The Gator stopped. Tucker's jaw dropped. "Will *talked?*"

"Nonstop."

"My son. Talked. With you. You're positive?"

She wanted to laugh. "I didn't do anything special. Except trust him. I told you last week that I'm the only one who handles the vanilla. Which is true. But that means sometimes I'm overwhelmed with the amount of work in the vanilla greenhouse, so I took him there, showed him what I was trying to do. And your Will— he just dove in, like a fish for water. He worked harder than me...and trust me, I can usually outwork any three people blindfolded and in my sleep."

Tucker still looked stunned. She wasn't sure he was listening. "Anyway, Will's welcome as many afternoons as he wants to come. I tried to give him an overview of the things I do, so he could pipe up if anything particularly interested him. The only concern I had was... well, he's still just ten. I don't want to overwork him. And I don't know if you want him on tractors or lawn mowers, that sort of thing."

By then Tucker had started the Gator again. They passed cabins, crossed over a wooden bridge, rode beside a diamond-dancing stream. Rhododendron draped the banks, their hot-pink flowers in full bloom, lush and rich. Garnet was still inhaling the views when Tucker finally turned the key.

"This is it. It's an observation tower, but we just call it the Tower. Special view from there. You're not afraid of heights, are you?"

She climbed off the Gator, viewed the eight sets of crooked stairs aiming mighty high. "No, not at all," she assured him…although the backs of her thighs creaked and groaned by the time she'd made it halfway, and the last quarter of climbing was sheer punishment. But then…they reached the lookout platform.

She had to swallow. They owned the mountain from here. A pair of eagles nested in a crevice of rock. The forest below glistened from the day's rain, making smells all fresh and sharp. Pine. Earth. Verdant sweetness. And far below, the view of blooming rhododendron was even more breathtaking.

"Magic," she said.

He leaned against the wooden rail. "Yeah. That's just how I feel whenever I come up here. It's good for anyone, everyone. Kids even forget they have a cell phone for a little while."

She cocked her head. "And I could stay here all night. It's beyond wonderful. But…somehow you're not mentioning how your afternoon went with my Pete."

"Yeah, well. Our afternoon didn't go so well."

Garnet couldn't guess what he was going to say, but Petie hadn't wanted to go home, had been chatting with Tucker ten for a dozen—so how bad could a problem be? And Tucker looked so right up here, with the wind combing through his hair, his skin all weathered… He had some dirt on him, no different than she did, but her draw toward him had nothing to do with scuffed shoes or hair that hadn't seen a brush in hours. He'd be arresting anywhere, in a tux or on a beach. He was so part of his sky-high mountain here. Wild. Free.

"Your son," he said, and sighed, the sound of a frazzled man. "I started with him in the office, only because I had to pick up some staff badges before a group of kids arrived. Unfortunately, the office was as far as I could budge your Pete."

"I tried to tell you he's not very motivated toward sports—"

"It had nothing to do with that. We never had a chance to even try any outside activities. He took one look at my office and said, 'Wow, you're even worse than my mom.'"

"Uh-oh," Garnet murmured.

"He said your office looked like heaps. Heaps of this and heaps of that. He said he was paying your bills on-line until you put a stop to it. He said—that you said—that shouldn't be his responsibility. Because he's a kid, and you're the adult."

"Well...I did say that. I mean, I'm doing okay, but I have cash-flow problems now and then. I didn't want him worrying about our finances, much less at his age."

"Hold it. I wasn't trying to pry. I was just trying to explain what happened. Your son took one look at the office, plunks down at *my* desk, in *my* office chair, with an expression like he just won the lottery." Tucker rubbed the back of his neck. His face expressed bewilderment at how things with her Petie could possibly have gone so wrong. "He was talking to me like I was the kid."

"Oh, well, he does that." Garnet added, "Pretty much all the time."

"My high-school group showed up. The summer staff was ready to take them on—but I always meet a new group up front, introduce myself, try to make everybody feel welcome and comfortable, give them the basic plan. Point being, I had to be out of the office for a little while. Say a half hour?"

"Uh-oh."

"When I came back…well, your son had phone messages tacked to the corkboard for me, with the time and the name and the message and the number. And then there was my desk. I didn't know it had a green slate top. I don't remember ever seeing the top of my desk naked like that before."

"Um…"

"Pete said he didn't have enough time to really case the place. That was his term. 'Case.' But he'd gotten on the computer, discovered the programs I had, went online, looked at the website. He said, not to insult me, but it was pitiful. Hey. Are you *laughing?*"

She couldn't help it. "I'm sorry," she gasped. "He shouldn't have been disrespectful. Honestly, he knows better—"

"He wasn't remotely disrespectful. He said over and over that he wasn't trying to insult me. Would you *quit?*"

But she couldn't seem to choke back the laughter. "You don't understand. It's such a relief. To have someone else—an adult—spend time with my son. I'm always blaming myself for his not being, well, like every other kid. For *his* sake."

"What are you talking about? He's terrific. Just because I wanted to knock his smart little block off doesn't mean I didn't get the picture. And I'm just saying. You have to give me time. He's smarter than me. I wasn't expecting that."

"Neither was I. He came out of the womb smarter than me."

"I *do* think he should get yanked out of the office and forced to have fun now and then."

"Good luck with that," she said wryly, and suddenly he leaned back, as relaxed as she was, and started chuckling along with her.

"This is *not* how I thought the afternoons with the boys would go."

"Me either! To be honest, I never thought this had a prayer of working. It just seemed too crazy an idea. For sure, there was no harm in trying it, but now..." She hesitated, then said more seriously, "I have no way of knowing if being around me will help Will. But I really, really like your son, Tucker. We had a great time together."

"That's how I felt with your Pete. I have no idea if I can get the kid into trying a sport or anything physical. I expected to challenge him—not for him to challenge me. But I had a blast, just talking to him, being with him. Which is to say, I'm 100 percent okay with our continuing this. As long as it works for the boys."

"As long as it works for the boys," she echoed.

A silence fell. She was still smiling—what a surprise, that she could be comfortable with Tucker. It mattered, that he liked her son. That she liked his. Talking about their kids had proved to be a natural anxiety squelcher.

But that easy silence seemed to fade away, turn into something else. She had the sudden urge to gallop down those long steps, grab Pete, get home, lock the doors. She wasn't in danger exactly. There was just something kindling in Tucker's eyes—a hot-blue, electric something—that had nothing to do with sons or parenting or anything sensible.

The sky seemed to hush. She started to say something, then stopped. She had nothing to say, no words in her brain that made any sense. Nerves tiptoed into her consciousness. Nerves, need...and a yearning, long ignored, long denied.

Something could happen here.

A touch. A kiss. Not because she'd been turned on by him from the first moment she saw him. But because he was looking at her that way. Like a man on the prowl. For her. The way a buck picked out a doe. The way an alpha male wolf chose his mate.

In that hush of a millisecond, she had a crazy instinct that something monumental, something overwhelming, something irrevocable, could happen if she did the wrong thing. That was the problem, of course. That she'd done so many wrong things already. That—except for Petie and Plain Vanilla—she had a long, long history of disappointing everyone in her life. Of making bad choices.

Yet…her heart was beating so fast, so hard, that it seemed like a raucous thrum in her ears. Only then she realized…there really was a raucous thrum. It emanated from the cell phone in his shirt pocket.

Tucker put on an ogre's scowl—but he plucked out the phone, saw the message, punched the thing. "Yeah. Of course. We'll be right there."

He snapped the thing closed, shook his head, stepped back. "That was the kids, naturally, wanting to know what's taking us so long."

There. The interruption was just enough for her to find a way to breathe again, to find some nice, normal words. "I'll bet. Our boys have to be starving."

"They're ten. They're always starving. You feed 'em and they're empty in an hour."

"You're not kidding. I swear Pete has a hole in his foot. He keeps taking in food and yet never seems to gain an ounce.…"

The whole climb down, they laughed that way, talking nonsense, telling son-stories. Tucker revved the

Gator to top speed to skedaddle home. They pulled into his drive less than five minutes later. Garnet could see the boys on the porch with Tucker's sister.

She quickly fished her van key from her shorts pocket. "So, we're going to try this again on Thursday?"

"Sounds great." Yet he suddenly reached out, hooked a hand around her wrist. The instant she glanced up, she saw that unpleasant, dangerous, unnerving glint in his eyes again. "Saved by the bell this time," he murmured.

"The bell?"

"All right. Technically you were saved by the phone. And I suspect it'll be tough working anything out with the boys around—and the boys are pretty much likely to always be around. But I'll find a way. Trust me."

She wanted to pretend she didn't know what he was implying, but she was shocked that he'd been so blunt, so daring. And in the next second, Petie came hurtling over, whining loudly about how starved to *death* he was, and when did he get to come back to Mr. Tucker's?

The group shared goodbyes, and faster than lightning, they were in the van and gone, first his house out of sight, then his road, and finally they were taking the hairpin turns toward home. Her son kept up his usual chatter. Relief slowly eased her runaway pulse. They'd been a family of two for so long. They'd been doing just fine, thriving in their two-against-the-world scenario.

She wasn't *really* worried about Tucker.

She'd learned from her mistakes in the past. Maybe she'd been a rebel as a kid…but now she colored between the lines. She no longer took risks she couldn't afford.

She just had to keep reminding herself of that.

Chapter Five

Tucker watched until they were out of sight. The sun was dropping fast now. A silken mist softened the edges of the woods and muted the sky colors, easing the way into night. In that prenight lonely silence, the mountain started to whisper.

Or maybe he just heard that unnerving whisper because he was thinking about Garnet.

He loped up the porch steps into the house. Inside, across the great room, he saw his sister and Will huddled over the kitchen counter—where they'd obviously been raiding the entire contents of his refrigerator.

"Help yourself," he said wryly.

Rosemary shot him a gesture that Will couldn't see. "I swear I won't stay long. But Ike called me yesterday. Told me I should check in with you when I could, or you'd start worrying."

"You think I worry about you?"

"Yeah, you've always been a total pest that way." She finished a spoonful of ice cream—peppermint stick, her favorite, which he just happened to always keep stocked. "I was fooling around the upper-east quadrant of Whisper this afternoon. I was so close, figured I might as well visit."

"I take it there's some weeds up there you're interested in?"

"Orchids, boy. Not weeds. Wild orchids. I pity you, having to live with him," Rosemary said to Will, who blushed to the roots of his hair.

Tucker stared at his son. Will used to be as easy around Rosemary as anyone alive. Yet when that last hormone spurt had kicked in, that changed, even with his one and only favorite aunt. Yet Garnet said he'd talked nonstop with her.

What was that *about?*

Tucker started with the older-brother grilling. "You talked to the parents recently?"

"Of course. They both call at least once a week. Always on the fly—you know they have no free time. They definitely don't want me to forget that they're still upset I canceled the wedding. That I hurt George irreparably. That nothing I'm doing makes sense these days. And right about then, the phone call invariably gets interrupted—usually by a page from the hospital—and I'm off the hook for another day."

She was being mighty flip, typical of Rosemary. But he was glad she stopped by, because she was incapable of asking for help from anyone. The only way he could know she was seriously okay was to get a look at her.

From the time Tucker was in grade school, he'd felt more like a father than a brother to both his siblings— but Rosemary especially. Their parents couldn't help being absent. They were both top surgeons in their field, always seemed to get called away. Tucker couldn't remember a birthday or a holiday where both parents were present. And that was all water over the dam, now that they were all grown.

But since running out on her fiancé, Rosemary had been trekking all over the mountains and woods, living solo, and being out of cell range for long stretches of time.

Of course he worried about her.

Something had gone way wrong with the guy she'd almost married. She was hurt. Bad hurt. She never said it. But her eyes looked lost, and she'd stopped confiding in anyone. Even him.

"Hey. Earth to Tucker." She rolled her eyes at him. "Whatever you were thinking about, quit it. What's with the lady?"

"What lady?"

"Give it up, Tucker. This is your sister. I heard the whole deal about the infamous and terrible Mrs. Riddle, and because of her, the boys get to do some new stuff this summer. I heard. Then I took the wax out of my ears, because there was certainly more to the story. Once I met her…well. You haven't looked at a woman that way in a long, long time."

"The boys are in the same class, for gosh sakes. They have been for a blue moon. Parents get to know each other."

"Oh, yeah." Rosemary nodded gravely. "That's why you were looking so gobsmacked. And just for the record, she was looking at you google-eyed too."

"She wasn't looking at me google-eyed. She's never looked at me google-eyed. Even once." When Rosemary didn't immediately shoot back something annoying and sisterlike, he glared at her. "What? What?"

"So that's how it is," Rosemary murmured.

"What is *that* supposed to mean?"

"Nothing." She stood up, leaving a counter-full of dirty dishes in her wake. "Will promised me a game of cards. After that, I'm headed home."

Maybe. He suspected she'd crash in one of the spare rooms if he pushed her to stay—which he would. Even when he was mad enough to strangle his sister—which happened often—his bond with her was still stronger than titanium.

He foraged for dinner, found more than enough to fill a plate. But his mind homed back on Garnet the minute he was alone.

There'd been an almost-kiss between them. An almost-embrace. He knew it. She knew it. Damned if he could figure out why he hadn't just taken the chance, pulled her in, forced both of them to figure out whether they actually had something together.

But he had the instinct that they did. Have something serious. Something so serious, so strong, that maybe there'd be no turning back once that door was opened.

That could be a good thing. A great thing. But there were just a few lines that Tucker never crossed. He'd been raised by a family who didn't put kids first, then married a woman who turned out to have the same flaw.

Tucker didn't mind trouble, didn't mind risk…and from everything he'd seen, Garnet was as crazy about her son as he was about his. But he took the *family* word seriously. He didn't do anything halfway, didn't want a halfway family.

Pretty insane to worry this early in the relationship,

but it was there. Tucker had no interest in playing unless the stakes were for keeps.

When another week had passed, Garnet figured she'd
been worried for nothing. Will came over on Thursday,
then Monday, then Tuesday again. Her Petie spent the
same afternoons on the mountain. She'd left messages
to let Tucker know what his son had been up to. He'd
left messages back about Pete.

She wasn't avoiding him. He didn't seem to be avoiding her. Summers were crazy busy for both. There was
no spare time to breathe—much less find time to do
silly stuff like, well, like date. Or fall in love. Or even
daydream about falling in love.

She woke up Thursday morning, bounced out of bed,
couldn't wait to face the day.

Right about that point, the day turned around and
became a nonstop debacle. First a bag of fertilizer broke
in the back of the van. Then Sally showed up for work
with bruises on her face and arms, wouldn't go home,
wouldn't go to the doctor, wouldn't call the police, just
dropped and broke about everything she touched. A tour
bus blew in—no warning, no planning—and that was
good. Sort of. Technically it was a mother lode of customers; it was just that the bus doors spilled out somewhere around fifty-five ladies, all wanting to wander
around and be waited on simultaneously. One had a
dizzy spell. Two needed their insulin refrigerated. Another lady needed first aid for a scratch and a blister.

She might as well have sold tickets to a frenzy, and
then midafternoon, out of the blue, Tucker called. Will
was with her that afternoon; Petie was still at Breakaway. When she grabbed the cell, she was so parched
she could barely find her voice.

"Garnet. I think we should talk. We haven't had a catch-up on the kids in more than a week."

"Sure," she said, and meant it. But there was something in his voice. Something besides the usual sexy tenor that knocked her socks off. "Something's wrong with Pete?"

"Nothing's wrong. But yeah, I do want to talk to you about him."

"Tell me now." Her worry button had been pushed. It was her mom worry button. Kind of like a siren that refused to shut off until she knew for positive he was okay.

"Can't."

He didn't explain. She credited him with having a reason. And it didn't matter what she had going on, if there was an issue with her son, that came first. "I close up shop here around six. But it's my turn to do the pickup on the boys—"

"I'll do it this time. And I'll bring some burgers or something. The boys will hopefully just hang for a while. We can just take a walk, get a conversation in that way."

"All right," she said, although she wasn't sure how she could possibly pull all her loose ends together by six.

But the craziness started to ease around five. She grabbed a few seconds to wash her face, put on lip gloss and brush her hair, but that was all the prep time she could manage. Even after the Closed sign was put in the window, the cash register had to be emptied, the cash and checks counted. Will *loved* counting money. They'd pulled up stools, leveled a half pitcher of lemonade, and both kept an eye out for Tucker's white truck.

A car pulled in a few minutes before six—not Tucker's truck, but a sleek silver Mercedes. The lady who stepped out was a beauty, a classic Charleston belle. She was slight in build, with a simple, perfect blond coif, a St. John outfit in white with navy trim and Italian white sandals. Her makeup was discreet, her posture perfect.

Garnet could see the wink of diamonds in the lady's ears and around her throat from a hundred yards away.

It was her mother.

Patricia Cattrell peered in the shop window, spotted her youngest daughter and strolled in with a radiant smile. "Oh, sweetheart, I missed you and Petie so much! Your daddy and I had a little surprise for you, and I just wanted to deliver it in person. It just seems like *ages* since you've been home—"

In two seconds, Garnet was enveloped in a hug of delicate perfume, then held at arm's length.

"Oh, my, you look so tired. I know you're working too hard. And I see that chin of yours going up. I know you're too proud to admit it. You wouldn't be a Cattrell if you didn't have a good dose of pride, honey. You're strong and proud and so beautiful—"

"Thank you," Garnet said swiftly, "But…"

"But honey, your skin. And I see callouses on your hands. And your face, no makeup, no moisturizer. And is that a terrible bruise I see on your calf?"

"It's nothing, Mom, I just—"

"Well, now, I do love your hair. It was always so thick, such a wonderful color, but bless your heart, I do think you need a little trim. And this is all going to come together, trust me—"

Garnet's heart suddenly thumped with alarm. "What is all going to 'come together'?"

"Why, the surprise your daddy and I have for you." Her mother stepped back, just long enough to open her snakeskin bag and pull out an envelope. "Four days in a spa in Charleston. Just for you. And I'll take Petie, so don't worry about that even for a second. I can't wait to have some time with my grandson, and your daddy feels the same way. It's just a little present for your birthday, honey, we wanted to give you something special—"

"My birthday isn't for a month, Mom. And I can't go anywhere right now and leave Plain Vanilla."

"Of course you can. It's just a shop. And the timing is precisely the point, honey. You're not getting any younger, bless your heart. You want to look your best, but that takes a little extra effort after the big three-oh. Now...where's my Peter? And who is this handsome young man?"

Garnet, always out of breath after a conversation with her mother, turned to find Will, hot red from his forehead to his neck, standing still as a statue and saying nothing.

"Garnet? Who is this young man? And, dear, I need to go into the house and freshen up...."

Garnet introduced Will, swooping an arm across his shoulder to give him something to lean against. Will was actually bigger than her—both in weight and height. But he had that gobsmacked look she knew well.

She felt gobsmacked after even short conversations with her mother.

"This is Will, Mom. Will MacKinnon. He's been working with me two or three afternoons a week." She gently put a little pressure on his right shoulder, trying to hint that he needed to extend a hand.

Which he did. Tucker had apparently taught him manners—even if he was overwhelmed by the company.

Her mom accepted the hand, shook it warmly. "Well,

it's very nice to meet you, Will. Is your daddy of the Walker MacKinnons?"

"No, ma'am. I'm of the Tucker MacKinnons. Walker is just my grandpa's name."

"Oh, my…" Her mom looked from Garnet to Will, back to Garnet, back to Will, speculation and calculation and questions in her eyes.

"No," Garnet said.

"Did I say something?"

"You were thinking about a question. And the answer is no."

"I was only thinking that Will comes from a lovely family. How nice that you—"

"No, Mom. *No*." She wasn't going to tear out her hair. She was just tempted to. Her mom only had to hear the landed-gentry MacKinnon name to picture weddings and stature and photos in the society columns and major jealousy at the country club. If Tucker had a clue what matchmaking devilment her mother could come up with, she'd be embarrassed out of her tree.

And that was when she heard the white pickup wheel into the drive.

Tucker was lost in thought when he turned into the Plain Vanilla parking lot. Next to him, Pete was happy as a clam, playing some game on a little machine and talking pretty much nonstop. "So I can change that on the website tomorrow, right?"

"Sure," Tucker said, not knowing what Pete wanted to do, but already dead sure the kid would be right.

Tucker wasn't used to being a failure around kids, didn't like the taste. All his life, he'd gone for challenges other people wouldn't even think of taking on. But getting Peter outside was harder than getting a Democrat to vote for tax cuts. He didn't say no. The kid was too polite for his own good. He was just like a miniature, quiet bulldozer, continuing on the path he wanted, and finding some way to duck anywhere Tucker tried coaxing him to go.

He had to have a sit-down with Garnet. Find some way to explain his failure without looking like either a failure or a slave driver. And he had another plan he'd like to put to her. The plan was totally about the boys, of course.

But—just by accident—it was a way to test how she really felt about family.

"So," Pete said, "there's no reason you couldn't show me your tax stuff. I *like* it. I know Mom's taxes. I know her tax program. That's not *work,* Mr. Tucker.... Uh-oh."

Tucker glanced at Peter, suddenly paying attention again. Two cars were leaving the Plain Vanilla parking area, leaving one still there. A bullet-silver Mercedes.

"What's the uh-oh?"

"That's my grandma's car." Pete let out an old-man sigh. "I love her okay. She really gives me neat stuff. And usually I go for two weeks with her and Grandpa. They take me all over the place. We have a great time. She says I can make her laugh like nobody else."

"So what's the uh-oh factor?"

"She's not nice to my mom." Pete looked out the truck window again. "This is not gonna be good. Hurry and park, okay? I gotta help her."

"I'll help her." Tucker didn't believe he was having this nature of discussion with a ten-year-old, but Pete suddenly studied him seriously.

"Yeah, maybe you could. Grandma's *nice,* you know. But she makes my mom cry. I mean later. Not when she's there. But later my mom will be really bad upset. Hey, there's Will." Pete reached for the door handle. "Hey, Mr. Tucker, don't tell my mom I told about her crying." And the instant he was out the door, he yelled, "Hey, Will! We got a heap of burgers and fries! You hungry?"

Chaos ensued—Tucker's favorite kind of chaos. Garnet charged out of the shop, trailed by her mother—it had to be her mother; she had the same slight build and elegant bones her daughter had, even the same glossy hair, although the mom had dyed hers a pale blond. Introductions were made—Patricia Cattrell readily agreed to stay for dinner, even if it was nothing more than fast food. The boys somehow made more noise than a rock band just carrying paper plates and drinks from Garnet's kitchen, everyone settling at the picnic table outside in the shade. The cat jumped on the table...the pregnant cat, the one Garnet was never going to own.

Garnet's mom seemed to blend right in—especially considering she was hardly dressed to sit outside at a picnic table, between the precarious sandals and fancy white outfit. Still, she laughed with Pete, made conversation with his Will, didn't blink when the first of two drinks spilled and lifted the cat to the ground, but without comment.

She made a point of sitting next to him, but then Tucker figured a mom would likely do that, want to know the details of why a guy was showing up on her daughter's doorstep. So he was grilled, in the usual Southern way, a delicate reference to his last name and family...then a delicate reference to her family's pedigree...then some bless-her-hearts and oh-mys and where did you say you went to school? That's such a fine son you have, why, honey, you must have gotten married before you were out of college....

He knew the patter. A long time back, he figured Southern women descended from native cannibals. They looked cuter. But they'd saw off your head and boil it, if you went after their young without proper credentials.

Garnet's cell phone rang twice, calls she clearly had to take, because she took the phone to the side of her house, away from the noise. One call concerned her, because Tucker could see her frown, see her rub the back of her neck.

The chaotic dinner abruptly petered out. The second spill had been orange juice, and some of it had spilled on Garnet, who promised to be back in less than ten, but it was so sticky she really needed to shower it off. Patricia gracefully got to her feet, said she had to go, but she needed a minute with Petie. Tucker and Will scooped up the debris from dinner...at least until Pete charged back in the door and said Will "and him" were going on a treasure hunt, and "it'd only take a couple of minutes, okay, Mr. Tucker?"

And yeah, it was okay with Tucker. In three minutes flat, the dinner messes were cleaned up. Garnet hadn't returned yet—no surprise, she was never going to shower and change in ten minutes, no woman could— so Tucker had a few minutes to test out the couch in her living room.

It was the first chance he'd really had to get a look at her place. The couch was a lot of years from new, but it was thick and cushy. She'd painted the walls a pale ocean-green, the trim white. The long east windowsill was luxuriously crammed with plants. A floor-to-ceiling bookcase was packed helter-skelter, lots of

nonfiction on plants and herbs and horticulture, all dog-
eared and well used, with a couple shelves of romances
and suspense. The hardwood floors were dusty, but an
area rug—a swirl of vanilla and teal—was soft and
plush. One wall had photos of Pete from the time he
was a baby.

She hadn't decorated with money. Just color and
comfort. The only item of real financial value was an
odd table at the far corner. Semicircular. Rich veneers.
Six-legged. An antique, Tucker thought. Unlike everything else, it was dusted and hand waxed and nothing
cluttered the top. So it was something she loved, he
mused. Everything else was something she could give
up or replace, but that table mattered to her somehow,
someway.

The boys suddenly surged from a back room, both
of them all excited, chattering nonstop.

"So…what was the treasure hunt about?" Tucker
asked.

"Money." Petie plopped onto the carpet, crossing his
legs. Will sprawled next to him.

"Wait until you see this, Dad," Will said.

"What?" Only his jaw dropped when he *did* see what
was in Pete's hands.

Not just money. But hundred-dollar bills. At least
ten of them.

"Wait until my mom sees this," Pete said. "She'll be
so upset, she'll be throwing things, I'm warning you.
It's not gonna be pretty. So if you guys want to get out
while you still can—"

Right. Like Tucker was going to leave without fig-
uring *this* out.

Chapter Six

Tucker was still talking to the boys when he heard Garnet's bedroom door open.

"Hey, guys, I'm sorry I took so long! But between the orange juice spill and the day's dirt, I really needed a scrubbing from head to toe…. Uh-oh. What? What's wrong?"

Tucker sucked in the look of her. She'd obviously hurried through a shower, not wanting to keep anyone waiting. Her face and feet were bare. She'd pulled on shorts and an oversized sweatshirt with the sleeves long torn off, the neckline droopy-loose, revealing delicate collarbones and the hollow in her throat. Somewhere inside had to be breasts, but whether she wore a bra or not was a tantalizing question.

The boys were standing next to him. Tucker wasn't supposed to be thinking about tantalizing questions.

But she was so naturally…earthy. Not put-on. She

was just sensuous to the bone, from her luminous eyes to her wildly exuberant hair, to that pulse, so delicate and vulnerable in her throat.

"Hey," she said, worry thick as honey in her throat now. "Something happened, I can see it in your face, Petie, what…? Oh."

The healthy color in her cheeks faded to chalk-white. He could see her gaze shoot to Petie's hands…to the splay of hundred-dollar bills. She surged forward, clasped the bills in a quick fist, at the same instant her posture straightened.

"I should have guessed what happened," she said cheerily to Pete, then smiled at him and Tucker both— but it wasn't a normal Garnet smile. It was an I'm-tougher-than-stone smile. "Well, now. Is anyone still hungry or need anything else to drink? I don't know how long Tucker and Will can stay—"

Tucker was ready with an answer. "I'm guessing we've all had a long day, but the boys were hoping to play just one game of *Wilderness*. Right, guys?"

Will glanced at him with a question in his eyes, but Petie said immediately, "Yeah. It won't take us more than an hour, I promise. Come on, Will."

"Yeah," Will echoed. The two boys thundered back to the computer room/den, making conceivably the same noise as a herd of elephants.

For the first time in a long time, they were alone. Garnet realized that even faster than he did…since she was looking as stubborn as a goat and as proud as a princess. She was still wearing that tinsel smile. "Well, are you still thirsty? I could probably scare up a beer if you—"

"Sure. What's the story about the money?"

"Hmm?" She'd already zipped across the room and

was bending into the fridge, rooting behind various fresh foods. "I've got a light or a regular. Only one can of each, though. I can't remember when I bought this. It had to be quite a while ago. I don't know if beer spoils. I mean, it could even be a year old or more—"

He wasn't buying the nonstop chatter. "Garnet. Pete said you'd be upset." A massive understatement, he thought now. Her voice was low and jittery. She was still frantically searching for that beer. And she'd put the hundred-dollar bills on the top shelf with the milk. Offhand, yeah, Tucker'd call that way upset.

"My son is such a tattletale." She gave up searching and brought out both cans, lifting one and then the other for his vote.

He stepped forward, removed both cans from her hands and elbowed the refrigerator door closed.

"You don't like either kind?"

"It's pretty unusual. Your son said he was going on a 'treasure hunt.' Then he comes back with Will holding a pretty amazing amount of money."

"I know, I know. I don't blame you for being curious. And I'll tell you, okay? But not when the kids are close or could hear. Petie thinks he knows everything. But there are some things—"

"Uh-huh." He set the beer cans on the counter, wrapped a cold hand around Garnet's wrist and herded her toward the door. It wasn't hard. She didn't have a lot of defenses right then. He could see that, which meant— by his guy code of right and wrong—that he couldn't and wouldn't take advantage.

But the instant he had her outside and the door closed…well. The evening heat seemed to go straight to his brain.

He happened to kind of lay her up against the door.

Then happened to kind of trap her with his arms, sealing her between him and the door. Then he looked at her, at her eyes, at her mouth. She opened her mouth to say something. Maybe.

Who knew what her intent was?

He'd covered her mouth by then.

Right off, right that second, that first kiss was exactly what he'd hoped for. Exactly what he'd been afraid of.

If she had defenses, she left them at the closed door. Inside the lady was a firestorm. Her lips were softer than butter, the hitch in her breath almost a hum, and before their tongues touched, she'd suddenly clutched his shoulders, as if afraid of falling.

He understood the fear, because he felt exactly the same. He could fall. She could fall. Maybe he was still the only one who knew it, but the grip on his shoulders turned into a slow slide around his neck. The deeper the kiss, the more she sank into him.

The more she sank into him, the more of her slim, lithe body touched his. Pushed his. Molded to his like puzzle pieces that wouldn't fit anywhere else, not like this, not this tight, this soft, this perfect.

When he lifted his mouth, she murmured something...maybe a silvery, whispery *whoa*...but unless she clarified that she wanted him to stop, he sure as hell wasn't.

The night had turned nightmare-black, not because it was so late, but because clouds were rolling in, dark and low, thrumming an uneasy atmosphere, sparking worry. In his pulse. In hers. Ah, yeah, this was danger. His hands took a slow, moody slide under the hemless bottom of her sweatshirt, found warm, damp skin.

Gradually his hand found the side of her breast, then sneaked over just enough to cup. Her nipple hardened in the heart of his palm, and her responsiveness went straight to his groin. He rubbed against her, feeling hotter and harder than a teenage boy. He'd forgotten how much it hurt.

There never was, never could be, a hurt this good, but he'd forgotten.

He'd done the celibate thing so long that his brain was only holding together by shaky threads. Or maybe it wasn't celibacy or hormones or lust rising hard and fast from the back closet. Maybe it was just Garnet. The textures and scents and tastes of her. Especially the textures. The endlessly soft slope of her breasts, then the slide-glide down her ribs, slipping just fingertips inside her shorts. He didn't feel panties. Didn't feel anything but the firmness of her fanny.

An amazement. How perfect her butt was. The slope. The shape. When he pressed, and her pelvis rocked against the hot steel trapped in his jeans, another switch short-circuited in his brain. He had to contort his whole body to make maximum contact. She was too darned short. It wouldn't matter in bed. It just mattered now, trying to make love to her against the rough side of a building. But right then, he wasn't about to change anything…except to shiver another kiss on her.

This kiss evolved, started out sweet and then turned into something deep and dark, the pressure of satin lips and the taste of longing. His whole life, he'd tried to be a good man, a damn good man, but right then…he'd had enough. The only thing that mattered was achingly simple. He wanted her. Period. Now. Fast. Hard. Any way. All ways.

"Tucker."

He heard her. But she was calling him, not stopping him. Her lips traced the side of his neck, up to the razor line. She kissed a spot that suddenly developed a pulse, a throbbing pulse, because her lips lingered and treasured and enticed. She talked to him with her kisses, with her touch. She…

Hell, he didn't know what he was saying. What he was thinking. There was no explaining his response to her.

There was nothing in his world like her. No one was like her.

A nasty thought tore to the surface…a cautionary thought that he did his best to ignore. This was too soon. Of course he knew that, of course it mattered. He needed to know what family meant to her, what a family could mean to her. He had to know what she wanted in the long run. If there was any chance her needs and wants could mesh with his own.

That stuff was important.

And he'd had a serious plan to be careful—to hold off on any physical shenanigans until they both had a clearer understanding of each other. It was a plan that made good sense. It was upright, clearly thought out. Protective of her. Of their boys. Of all of them.

He remembered that part. That his plan was excellent.

Only just then, he wasn't thinking with his brain. He never wanted to see his brain or experience a rational thought ever again. The smell of her hair was so lush, so silky. Everything about her smelled just a little like vanilla. Nothing quite like vanilla. It was both a taste and a smell, an aroma you could inhale and wished you could keep on breathing in.

Like her. He just kept wanting to breathe her in. His palms slid deeper into her shorts, encountered… thong. There was no better underwear concept ever made. Whoever talked women into wearing thongs was brilliant. They were no impediment at all. Just a lusty teaser.

"Tucker."

Her tone wasn't a lover whispering this time, but quiet and real. He got it. He was going to have to get a grip. Maybe. He slipped his hands out of her shorts, since that behavior had provoked her suddenly cautious tone. He started rubbing and kneading her back instead. Heat shimmered between them, slick and fever-hot now.

Miserably hot now.

"Tucker."

"Just a little more. I promise I'll stop."

From nowhere, a throaty chuckle. "That's what the boys said in high school."

"You think I haven't matured beyond that?"

"Um. At this moment, no. I wouldn't trust you further than I could throw you."

"I think that's the real issue here. You could throw me. Maybe you already *did* throw me."

"I think you're stalling."

"Me? I'm pretty sure those are your hands still on my butt."

"That's completely accidental."

"Oh, yeah?" He wasn't regaining sanity. Didn't want sanity. But somehow, even ready to go off like a firecracker, he was calming down. Damn woman. She'd made him smile. Kept making him smile. "You think we could just stay here all night? Like this? Just teasing each other until the sun comes up?"

"You don't think you'd get tired?"

"There's no chance in heaven or hell that I could get tired. Not holding you."

A silence fell. She lifted her head, so her eyes could

meet his in the darkness. Her hands slid away from his behind. "What are you trying to do to me, Tucker MacKinnon?"

"If you don't know, I must not be doing it very well. But to give myself an excuse, it's been a long time. I tried to give it up completely after the divorce, but couldn't quite make that work. Even so, I know I'm way out of practice. Next time we do this, I'll—"

"You're giving me a whole lot of information there, Tucker. You sure this is stuff you want me to know?"

"Oh, yeah, I'm sure."

"So you think there's going to be a next time."

"Definitely. And soon. Don't you?"

She eased out from under his arm. He wished it weren't so damned dark. He couldn't see her expression clearly enough to interpret what she was feeling. "I want to laugh, Tucker. And I want to say yes. But here's the thing. I'm not looking for marriage for a really simple reason. I'm no good at it. And having kids our age—boys who see everything, who are curious about everything sexual—means it's just about impossible to have a sexual connection without marriage. So...I'm going in the house now. I'm going to rouse the boys. Close up for the night."

She didn't *run* into the house, but she escaped too fast for him to argue with her or analyze what she'd said. The boys showed up before he'd even caught his breath. Both were whining and complaining about being interrupted, it wasn't late, it wasn't fair, what was so special they had to stop the game that *instant* and Will totally didn't want to go home yet.

"I have a plan," Tucker suggested. That got no one's attention, so he said it louder.

That made Will turn, hunch his shoulders. "Uh-oh. It's always trouble when my dad gets a plan."

"I'm starting to learn that," Garnet said, innocent as sunshine—when there were two boys standing in front of her, priceless chaperons.

"Well, here's the plan. I was going to suggest it to Pete's mom first, but hey, it's up to all four of us. It's not easy to carve out any free time in the summer, but I think I could wrangle a long afternoon next Tuesday. If Pete's mom could do the same…well, I was thinking about a kayak race. Two teams. Winners get a serious prize."

Tucker saw Garnet's immediate frown. Yeah, he knew she had the shop, that summer was her bustling season, no different than his. But sometimes, family had to come first. At least it did for him. And provocative attraction or not, he needed to know it did for her.

Besides. He'd failed every other way to get Pete to do a sport or much of anything outside. So now he was reduced to bribery and manipulation. That wasn't how he liked to operate, but dagnabbit, sometimes the ends really did justify the means.

"Mr. Tucker, I've never even been in a kayak," Pete said, wearing his old-man worried look.

"I know that. But here's the thing. We'd set up the race so it was an even match. You'd be my crew, Pete. And your mom would be Will's crew. That way, both teams would have a novice kayaker and an experienced one. It'd be fair competition for both sides."

Pete was still frowning, but Tucker could see he was considering it. "I can swim. In fact, I can swim really well. But is it hard to kayak?"

"It can be. But I'll pick a kayak run that won't be too hard for anyone."

Pete wasn't quite ready to give up that frown yet. "So what's the prize for the winners?"

Hell. Tucker hadn't thought that far ahead—but he knew the prize had to be a stunner or the plan would never work. "A hundred-buck gift certificate at Best Buy. The winner is the winning kid—although the adults can veto an inappropriate purchase. Otherwise, it's whatever the winner wants."

"I'm in," Pete said immediately.

"I'm in," Will said, just as fast.

"I'm obviously in, since it was my plan. Garnet?" For the first time since their embrace, he looked at her.

Her lips still looked kiss-plumped and pink, her neck still impossibly vulnerable…but her expression had turned careful. Crystal-sharp careful. "I'm feeling ganged-up on," she said.

"Yeah, so?"

"Yeah, so, I think you should have brought up the plan with me first."

"You're right. I should have. But the thing is…either the idea works for all four of us, or it doesn't work at all. I mean, if either of the kids doesn't want to do this, I don't want to force-feed the idea. So there just seemed no reason to—"

"We want to do it," Pete said firmly. He was all but salivating at the vision of the money he could spend in Best Buy.

"Yeah, that's a big 'me, too,'" Will said.

"Tucker, you are an evil, evil man," Garnet pronounced.

"Is that a yes or a no?"

She sighed. "I'll have to make sure my staff are both here and can take over. I don't want to be the bad guy if there's some crisis I can't help with. And if there's a threat of storms—"

Tucker looked at the boys. "Yeah, yeah. That's obviously a rain-check kind of deal. So let's hear a straight yes or no."

He knew she'd go for it. He saw how she looked at Petie, how excited he was. That sealed the deal. So she *was* willing to put family before her work, which mattered to him more than anything he could say.

He was beyond-belief curious about those hundred-dollar bills—but when push came to shove, that was just a mystery. Nothing that really mattered.

The following Monday night, Garnet jerked awake at the unexpected chime of her cell phone. She groped in the dark for it on her bedside table, found it, dropped it, and with one eye open, saw 1:00 a.m. on the bedside clock. She bent over, felt with her hands, found the phone, slapped it open.

"Sally?" She could see the name on the phone, felt an immediate ball of thorns form in her stomach.

"Yeah. It's me. I know you need me tomorrow—you and Pete are going on that kayak thing."

"What happened. Where are you." This had happened too many times before for Garnet to phrase questions.

"In the hospital. I'll get out in a couple days. But I'm afraid I can't—"

"How bad?"

"Two bruised ribs. Nothing too bad. But when I fell down the stairs, it seems I did something to my right ear. Burst an eardrum or something."

"Another fall, huh? From a one-floor apartment." Garnet closed her eyes. "Oh, honey. When are you going to shake that guy?" But she backed off from that line immediately. "You need me to come?"

"No. And the doc says, even with the eardrum problem, I'll be better and back at work by Friday."

"Okay. Tell me if you need anything. I'll visit you tomorrow."

They talked a few minutes more, then Garnet clicked off the phone. She sat in the dark, not likely to fall back to sleep, unsure whether she should call Tucker this crazy late, or wait until tomorrow to cancel their kayak outing.

She hated to call him this late. He had to be sleeping. But she knew he'd had to rearrange schedules and employees for the kayak thing tomorrow. If it were her, she'd want to know the change in plans as soon as possible.

So she phoned. He immediately answered in a rusty, sleepy voice.

"Has to be you. You're canceling for tomorrow."

She was startled that he knew why she was calling. "Yes. I'm sorry. Please tell Will I'm sorry, too. I didn't have a choice—"

"You don't need to give me a reason, Garnet. I expected it. See you when we trade the boys next time."

She heard a click. It was more like a plunk than a downright slam. Still. He'd ended the call more than abruptly, and she stared at the phone for several moments before leaning back, wide-awake now and confused by Tucker's comments. He'd been sleeping, of course. He might have been disoriented or not thinking normally.

But the word *expected* kept replaying in her mind. He'd *expected* her to cancel their kayak outing? *Expected* her to let the kids down?

What was *that* about?

She'd never had the chance to mention her employee being in the hospital. He couldn't possibly guess something like that was going to happen. She hadn't known. No one could have known.

So what Tucker must have *expected*...was that she'd let him down.

Two mornings later, Tucker was leading a rambunctious group of sixty-five boys on Snake Trail. The kids were twelve- and thirteen-year-olds—which meant they were as easy to control as a pack of hyenas. The trail was a three-mile hike around the east side of the mountain, included some boulder-climbing and slinking through a couple of narrow canyons.

Tucker loved it because it invariably took some of the sass and starch out of a wild group. They loved it because of the name. A six-foot snake had been spotted on the trail maybe five or six years ago. The unwitting snake had become a legend that the next group of kids always heard about. The boys always hoped there'd be another snake that big...or preferably bigger.

He turned around when he heard the buzz in his pocket, grabbed his cell, used the pause to turn around and survey the strung-out gaggle of boys. All of them looked capable of causing murder and mayhem. And likely would. But temporarily they were all hiking, even the stragglers.

His cell took the message. Just a short one. A velvet voice, saying, "I could tell you were annoyed the other night."

He hit her number, texted, Not.

She texted back. Yeah, you were. Is there a reason you don't want to explain why you were so irritated?

He didn't answer. Couldn't. The last kid in line—
who was at least sixty pounds overweight, and over-
dressed for a holy-hot day—went down like a sinking
rock. Hard to believe the boy could suffer heat exhaus-
tion this quickly, but something, for damn sure, was
wrong, and Tucker went running.

Late that same afternoon, Garnet finally managed
to trap Sally in the back room.

"I'm all right. I keep telling you. I don't need to be
coddled."

"I'm not coddling you," Garnet lied. "I need you to
help me with this, because I just can't get the time to do
it. And you've got an artsy streak that I'll never have."

"There's a hundred real things that need doing—like
mowing. Like bundling herbs. Like—"

Every job Sally named involved bending and twist-
ing. As beautiful as she was, her dark chocolate face
had looked almost white since she'd shown up for work
yesterday. The son of a sea dog had taken two teeth this
time. The right side of her mouth looked like an overripe
plum. She'd come to work in a giant-size man's shirt—
all the better to hide swelling and bruises.

Sally said she'd left the creep—but Garnet had heard
that story before. Every time she hoped Sally meant it,
but in the meantime, all she could do was give Sally
work she could handle and offer support.

The project was a poster, in the form of a burnt-edge
rustic slash of pine.

An overlay of white made for easy-to-see printing.
Special Uses for Vanilla was already stenciled at the top.

Sally read off the list Garnet wanted added to the
poster. "'When you're painting a room, add a couple
tablespoons of vanilla to the can to make the unpleas-

ant paint smell disappear.' You can really do that? 'Add ground vanilla to baked goods.' Hmm. 'Vanilla absolute is the highest concentrated extract of vanilla—and costs a fortune, so it's used in expensive perfumes.'" She looked up. "I never smelled vanilla in a perfume."

"It's in quite a few. But it doesn't smell like cooking vanilla in that form."

"Well, hey." Sally lowered her head again, and read further. "'Artificial vanilla extract isn't made from vanilla. It's made from vanillin...but also from ingredients like pine sap, clove oil and lignin—which is a waste product from the manufacture of paper....' All right, all right. I admit this is more interesting than I thought. Customers'll get a kick out of some of this."

"That's what I thought," Garnet said, feeling relieved Sally was buying in to the project. Her cell vibrated as she hiked back into the shop. She noticed Mary Lou take on two guy customers, who were clearly husbands looking for something their wives wanted.

She clicked on the phone, smiling as she stepped outside.

Tucker's voice was low and quiet, yet seemed to suck up all the oxygen in her sphere. She leaned against an outside bench, hiding in the shade.

"I'm sorry if I sounded ticked. The truth is, I thought you were running," he said...as if he expected her to remember their texts from this morning.

Which she did, every word, every nuance, every inflection. "You thought I was running from the chance to go kayaking?"

"Come on. You know I didn't mean that. I thought you were using an excuse. To pull back. From me. From us. From what seems to be building between us."

"I canceled because I had a sick employee. Sally. She called from the hospital in the middle of the night."

She heard him clear his throat. "Well, damn. I'm sorry. More than sorry. I'm sorry I got sharp, and sorry I didn't believe you."

Well, if that wasn't the most unfair thing on the planet. Damn man was so honest that he forced her to be honest, too. "It's 100 percent true, about canceling because of Sally. But...what you thought was true, too. I'm...worried about where the two of us are going."

"You think you're alone?"

"Tucker. I'm as far from an Ole Miss sorority girl as you can get."

"Huh? Didn't we already cover this? I married the traditional Southern belle. The marriage was as much fun as being tarred and feathered. Trust me, I'll never be looking for a repeat."

She heard the wry tone in his voice, and yeah, he was funny. But he hadn't seemed to hear her concern before—and she didn't think he got it this time, either. "Let me tell you about the hundred-dollar bills," she said seriously.

"I didn't ask."

A fat, black-and-yellow bumblebee hovered by the shop screen door. Another car pulled into the yard— three women, shoppers. The ball of fur—the pregnant cat that wasn't hers—was snoozing in the sun. Had to be a hundred degrees out. Damn cat didn't have a lick of sense.

"Ever since Petie was born—even before Johnny died—my mother would drive over, a couple times a year, set up this 'treasure hunt' where I'd run across hundred-dollar bills all over the house. Usually there was a thousand dollars."

"Okay," he said, as if prodding her to continue.

"I gave them back. She'd just do it again. When Pete got old enough to understand what money was, she made him part of it. It was fun. The treasure hunt. For him. For her. Just not for me."

There was a silence on the other end, then another quiet "okay."

"I stopped giving it back. There was no point. So every time, I put it in an account, for Pete's college. I put her name, Pete's name and my name on it. So she can take it back anytime she wants. And in the meantime, I've got a darned nest egg for Pete's college."

"No wonder you're unhappy. This sounds awful."

Okay. He made her smile. A short smile, but still a smile. "It's about trust, Tucker. Respect. My parents had two perfect daughters, and then there was me. Got pregnant the first time I slept with a boy, ran off and married him on high-school graduation night. Nothing was right between Johnny and me. My sisters both have master's degrees. I finished high school by the skin of my teeth."

"I'm still listening."

"My mom—and my dad—don't believe I can take care of my son financially for a second. They're very generous. And no one yells at me. It's just there. I'm not the black sheep, exactly. It's more... Somehow a weakness crept into the gene pool. My sisters and mother are gorgeous. I'm ordinary. The rest of the family talk up investments and 401Ks. I struggle to make payroll. They all have gorgeous homes. I started out with a leaky roof and furniture from Goodwill."

"Garnet."

"What?"

"You're not envious of them."

"Good grief, no. I want what I have. What I've built myself. I just need you to know, I guess, that I'm not close with my family. I'm not sure I even know what it takes to be close in a family. I love my son more than my life. But I haven't felt a pull for a man in a long time, Tucker. And I don't want to fail you. *Or* me. And it's worrisome, because I don't have any credentials in the family or marriage arenas."

"Okay. Is that completely off your chest now?"

"Yes."

"So we'll try for another kayaking race. *Next* Friday."

"Okay." She cleared her throat. "Did you hear me, Tucker?"

"I did," he said, and then clicked off.

Sally called from inside the store; a customer on the landline had a question. Garnet hustled back in, but the sound of Tucker's voice was still in her head. She'd wanted to be honest with him, about who she was for real, the kind of mistakes she'd made, no prettying up the picture.

It wasn't that she wanted to put herself down.

She just wanted to leave him a way out, if he wanted one.

Before either of them had gone too far.

Chapter Seven

The next Friday dawned, hot and bright. Not a cloud in the sky. No emergencies showed up over breakfast, and Pete was as revved up as an overstoked hot rod. "What time are they coming?"

"Eleven. The same time I told you ten minutes ago."

"But they could come early."

"That's true. But I doubt they're coming two hours early, Pete."

Two hours later, Pete was lying flat on the front porch, the reprobate cat purring on his bare stomach. He was wearing a bathing suit, Crocs, his life vest, heaps of sunscreen and a straw hat—for effect. He had a bag next to him, had packed three or four times now. A change of clothes, a towel, more sunscreen, three bottles of water, plastic-locked snacks, bug repellent, a bug bite stick, Garnet's cell phone. He'd been prepared since five that morning.

Garnet had managed to put on a dark green bathing suit, nylon shorts and a sleeveless cover. She'd twisted her hair up and clipped it, applied sunscreen. But she couldn't find her shoes or her wallet or her cell phone, and the MacKinnons were due any minute.

"Your water shoes are in the laundry room, Mom."

"Why on earth would they be there?!"

"Because you left them there."

"I know where the house keys are," she began, then saw her son—her bad, evil, wicked son—raise a lazy hand and jingle the set of keys. She popped outside to grab them, and tickle her son...just as an old Volvo pulled into the yard.

The car was nothing like Tucker's truck, but Tucker and Will climbed out, accompanied by an unfamiliar man—not that Garnet needed more than two seconds to identify him. He had blonder hair than Tucker's, had to be younger by several years, but he had the same strong-boned face, the same long, lanky build.

"Ike," he said, introducing himself before Tucker had a chance. "I'm the younger brother. The doctor. And just for the record, if I were interested in a woman, I'd likely do something like dinner and wine in the moonlight. Not drag her on some godforsaken kayak race in the middle of this heat." Ike shook his head. "My brother just doesn't know how to treat a woman."

Garnet had to smile. His handshake was warm and easy, just like his whole manner. "I can see why your brother never mentioned you before."

"Yeah, he likes to keep me hidden. Which is what I'm doing today—being your invisible behind-the-scenes guy. Tucker's truck is already at the base of the river. I'm driving you all to the top, where you pick up the kayaks."

"You could let me get a word in," Tucker mentioned. When he came up behind his brother, Garnet could so, so see the difference.

Both MacKinnons were good-looking beyond what was fair, but Ike had a kindness and quiet about him. Tucker was the one with the edges and dark corners. The sexiness. Or maybe that was her perception, because she could feel her body trying to glom toward him like a star for its sky.

"You don't need to get a word in," Ike told his brother. "Here's the plan, Garnet. I'm babysitting Tucker's mountain while you four are on this kayak trek. And since Tucker made me drive all this way to do that, I'm going to stay the night, which means I get my nephew for the evening. Your Pete's welcome to join us. Not sure whether we'll do a movie or a campfire or what, but we're aiming for something Tucker won't approve of."

Garnet glanced at her son. She could see Pete was interested in this idea, was already warming to Ike...but that wasn't enough to sway Garnet quite that fast. "Let's see how the day goes, okay? How tired we all are."

"And who wins," Pete reminded her.

That was the thing, Garnet thought. Both kids could win from this outing. Pete was happy to be with Tucker, and was doing something outdoorsy. Will, being Will, had a naturally more easygoing nature...but he was still beaming, looking forward to this.

She was the only antsy one in the group, although she was doing her best to hide those nerves. She wasn't afraid of hard work or heat. She could swim, knew she was basically strong and fit. She really didn't know what was causing the clutch in her pulse, but she couldn't seem to shake it.

Around an hour later, they reached the portage site,

and Ike dropped off the four of them. The kids were beside themselves with excitement.

"I know exactly what game I'm going to buy when Mr. Tucker and I win," Pete told her as they finished donning life vests and organizing their gear.

She kept studying the kayaks, which were all bright-colored and mighty small and looked as if they could tip over for a breath of wind. Thankfully there wasn't much wind, just a whisper unsettling the tall pines bordering the river and a blaze of midday sun.

"This is pretty awesome, huh, Mom?"

"Yeah, way awesome," she agreed. The water was rushing from above, making a noise like thunder, looking like a streak of white diamonds pouring down. Below, she could see boulders and rocks in the water. Boulders they could run into. Sharp, hard rocks that seemed to be everywhere.

"Hey." Tucker disengaged from the boys, hooked an arm around her shoulder, steered her a few feet away. "Garnet, if you don't want to do this, we can call it off right now. It was just an idea. That's all. I've been struggling to find ways to encourage your Pete to do something, anything, that remotely resembles a sport…but this was only one idea. I'll find others. We'll find others. If any of us are afraid, it totally destroys the fun factor. So if you want to—"

"I'm not afraid," she said immediately.

"Will's done this since he was five years old. And the river's shallow here, almost never deeper than waist-high. The current's fast, but you could jettison the kayak at any time, probably be able to stand up—"

"I'm a decent swimmer. Pete's a good one. And I love the outdoors, Tucker. I'm no sissy."

"I know that." But he kept studying her face. "You're sure you want to do this?"

Of course she was sure. If it didn't work, she'd be dead and wouldn't know the difference. Every impulsive decision she'd made in the past had pretty much ended in disaster...but this was for Pete, not her. This was about Pete, not her.

The two kayaks lined up. Tucker gave some instructions, laid out some ground rules. "It's the law of the water. Anyone's in trouble, the other stops to help. Anyone has a problem, we all stop. I'm guessing the course will take us a couple hours."

"And we're gonna get *way* wet!" Will enthused. "C'mon, Mrs. G. My dad and Pete don't have a chance. Not against *us!* I'll show you everything you need to know! C'mon! Hop in!"

She hopped in, following all orders—including removing her top so she'd have something dry to put on when the race was over. Good thing she'd been told that, because they barely shot from the starting line before they were caught in a swift current.

Will started paddling like mad...and the rollercoaster ride began. Around a giant boulder, down an angle, and suddenly there was a blast of sharply cold water in her face. She was drenched so fast, she could only gasp...and then unwillingly laugh.

Will laughed, too. "Isn't it great, Mrs. G.? Don't you love it?"

She wasn't sure what all that initial anxiety was about, but maybe what it took was that wild splash of cold water. "More than great. How fast do you think we can make this thing go?"

"Way fast. You ready?"

"You bet!"

Downstream they went, past boulders, then a fast slide and wild whoosh of water that drenched them both. From somewhere close, she heard Pete's yelp of laughter, Tucker's voice boisterously expressing exuberance and encouragement.

Their kayak surged ahead...temporarily. The Tucker/Pete team was never far. Garnet picked up the rhythm of the paddling. It wasn't just about speed, but about being in sync with Will—so the paddling had a music to it, a work-together pacing. Will was extraordinarily strong for a boy, and she might not have paddling muscles, but she was physically fit from her own work.

Her sun hat flipped off, lost in the churn and bubble of the river. As cold as the water was, the sun still beat down hotter than fire. Under a heavy canopy of trees, the deep shade provoked a shiver...but they were back in the sun within seconds. Her arms tired, ached, and still she kept up the pace.

Again, Tucker and Petie pulled up close. "Make way, you devils, for the faster team," Tucker yelled out.

"Yeah, Mom, we're gonna clean your clock!" Petie yelled out.

She whipped her head around, just to make sure it was really her son screaming out insults and challenges, soaking wet, having fun—being *outside,* doing a *sports* thing, and from the grin on his face, as their kayak passed hers, he'd forgotten all about the prize. He was having fun. Just plain old having fun.

"Eat my dust, Mom! Eat my dust!"

She and Will poured out more effort—at least she did. For the first time since they started, Will seemed to lose steam.

"Are you tired?" she asked him.

"Naw. They just picked up the current at the right time. But we can catch up."

They came close. As close as the length of three kayaks. And when she realized they couldn't win, she told Will, "I'm sorry I wasn't strong enough—but I'll find a way to make it up to you for the prize."

"Are you kidding? I didn't care about the dumb prize. I just want the four of us to get to do this again."

Will was still talking as they sort of soft-crashed into the sandy shore. Pete and Tucker appeared to be doing a victory dance. Will started laughing.

Garnet crawled out of the kayak and splayed, tummy first, on solid ground.

Eventually she was surrounded by the guys.

"Are we alive?" Tucker asked delicately.

"No. Five minutes from now, I'll be alive. Right now…not."

"Are we feeling just a little sad because we beat the pants off you?"

"You did *not* beat the pants off us. You won by a measly few yards. So maybe you get the prize this time, but I think Will and I want to demand a rematch. Will…?"

"Yeah, we want a rematch. Same teams. Same money. Different winner."

Will picked up a chant with that general refrain.

"If you guys are thirsty, there's some lemonade in the cooler there…."

The boys were off and running. Other people ambled around, some having finished a kayak or canoe or raft run, some waiting for family or friends to be picked up. She only saw Tucker. First his knees, kneeling next to her. His scrappy old khaki shorts. A yellow

T-shirt molded to his chest. All of him still dripping, just as she was.

"Tucker?"

"What?"

"This was a stupendous idea. Thanks for thinking of it."

"You're welcome."

"But I have to tell you something."

"What?"

She lifted her tired head, saw the boys were several yards away, turned a serious look back to Tucker. "Your son pulled back. He'll deny it, but he did. He let you and Petie win."

"Yeah, I know. I watched him. He's got a good heart, my kid, doesn't he?"

"A huge heart. What a kind thing to do."

"For God's sakes, don't let on you know." He made her swear, cross her heart, hope to die. When she rolled her eyes skyward at the silly childhood vow, he said, "Will and I talked about it last night. About how Pete likely never had an opportunity to win at any sport before. And we could do this again, so it wasn't as if either team only had one shot at winning. But that's as far as the talk went. I didn't suggest he do anything. I just wanted him to think about it."

She had to break away from the intense look in his eyes. A look that had nothing to do with children and kayak racing, and everything to do with two soaked adults, wearing nominal clothes, feeling the heat of the sun warm them up fast.

Or maybe it was the other kind of heat kindling all that warmth.

She forced her attention on the boys, who were slugging down lemonade at the speed of sound. "I'm kind of amazed at how well they get along, aren't you? They don't have much in common."

"Except for both being ten. And to be honest..." He hesitated.

"What?"

"I have this feeling they're plotting something."

"Like what?"

"I don't know. But they both stop talking when I come within hearing distance."

"Maybe, but what could they possibly be plotting?"

"Trouble." Again he caught her gaze, held it. "My son's almost as good at trouble as I am."

Her hair was tangled and wet, her nose undoubtedly beet-red from the sun, and she'd pulled on shorts over her bathing suit, but still, she was mostly bare. And vulnerable. Just the way he looked at her made her feel intensely vulnerable. Intensely naked.

"Hey, Dad...?"

Tucker looked up, arched an eyebrow at her, as if to say, "so much for adult time."

They scooped up all their heaps of gear, stashed everything in the back of his truck. The boys tumbled into the backseat, and she took the front seat next to Tucker.

Before they were halfway home, she turned to the backseat and said, "All right. What's wrong with you two?"

"What? What?" Petie said.

"I don't know what you mean, Mrs. G."

The innocence on both their faces was darned near frightening. "Neither of you have said a word. Now, what's going on?"

"Nothing," Will said. "Except that my Uncle Ike said we could both stay over tonight with him, like we told you. And we both want to do it. I told Pete about my uncle. Uncle Ike is awesome sometimes. Especially when we get him away from other adults and we just get him for ourselves."

"Yeah, and Mom," Petie added, "he's a doctor. So if anything happened, he'd be right there, you know. You wouldn't have to worry."

Garnet said to Tucker, "Something's going on here."

"Mom. There's *nothing* going on."

"Cross my heart, Dad. Like, come *on*. We're being quiet, so, like, now you're suspicious? How unfair is that?"

"Okay, okay, I apologize," Garnet said, and turned to face the front again—after a quick shared glance with Tucker. *Something* was going on. Pete hadn't even mentioned racing to Best Buy with his big win. That was like expecting peace in the Middle East. His mind had to be majorly occupied elsewhere.

But neither boy was prone to lie or cause trouble, so there wasn't much else she could do or say. At least right then. Tucker had barely pulled into his drive before the boys leaped out, running straight to Ike—who was standing on the top step of the veranda, waiting for them.

"We seem to have lost popularity," Tucker said wryly.

Garnet laughed. "I'll say. They both take to your brother like ducks to water."

"Ike's low-key. Never met a kid who didn't like him. I swear they'd follow him like the Pied Piper."

"But he's not married?"

"Not yet. At least that I know of. Ike plays his cards close to his chest, as far as his private life. Rosemary's been known to sit on him, ply him with liquor and force some news out of him, but it's always like that. Having to pull teeth."

"You think it runs in the family?"

He shot her a glance. She shot him an innocent smile right back, but he wasn't buying that innocence business, not anymore.

They popped out of his truck, grabbing gear, Ike and the boys helping, all of them chattering at once—messages for him, what had happened at the camp, where Ike was taking the boys that evening, all that general chatter. He kept one eye on Garnet.

She'd chosen to wear a modest one-piece bathing suit and a nylon pair of navy shorts for both modesty and cover. Her hair had gotten as soaked as the rest of her. She'd pulled it back in a crazy twisty ponytail, with sunglasses stuck on top. Her nose and shoulders were pink, but the rest of her had just gotten a little extra coat of sun.

Not that he actually had a vote, but personally he thought she was the sexiest woman alive, just as she was, natural and unconcerned about whether her hair looked just so or if there was a little sand between her toes.

"All right," Ike told them. "Boys and I are taking the Gator. We have enough food for six weeks, but if we run out before midnight, we'll likely come down to raid the refrigerator again. I've got fresh batteries in the walkie-talkie. We're staying in the top cabin, which probably means the altitude's too high for copperheads, but all three of us hope we see a bear. We intend to tell ghost stories, stay up as late as possible and do some other things that you two likely won't approve of. I'll bring them down the mountain by around nine tomorrow morning. Is there anything else you overprotective parents need to know?"

"Hey." Tucker clearly objected to being called over-protective.

"Hey," Garnet echoed him.

All the noise disappeared the instant the Gator was out of sight, leaving the two of them standing in the driveway. Every instinct warned Tucker to behave cautiously. "I'll take you home if you want," he said, "but since you're here…I'd like you to come in, see the old family homestead while I rustle up some dinner. We both have to eat."

She hesitated—as he'd guessed she would. "Tucker, I'm pretty beat, and I really need to shower off—"

"Yeah, so do I. But there's three full bathrooms—I can loan you an old T-shirt and short-sleeved sweatshirt, and you already have shorts."

"Well…"

"You probably don't like lasagna. My sister made a pan when she was here, which is no guarantee it's edible. She puts junk in there like herbs and all kinds of cheeses—"

"I'll stay until just after dinner," she said firmly.

"Sounds good. I'll pop dinner in the oven. We'll both have time to clean up."

He gave her the downstairs bathroom—because it was usually the cleanest—and scrounged up some fresh gray towels. "I think we started out with some other color towels down here, but ever since Will developed an addiction to dirt, gray just seemed the easiest. Beats me where he inherited that from. And yeah, I know this T-shirt will be swimming-big on you, but it's old and soft. Okay, here's a brush, some shampoo stuff…I don't know what else you might want, but just open some cupboards and drawers if you need something, okay?"

"Okay. Thanks," she said, as she gently, but firmly, shut the door in his face.

Possibly he'd been hanging too close. Thinking what it'd be like to shower with her. Thinking what they could do in a shower. Or a bath. Or both.

Possibly she'd suspected what he was thinking, and that was why she'd closed the door in his face. But she was still here, wasn't she? Wary and worried, but still here.

And there wasn't a kid in sight.

Whistling, he popped the lasagna into the oven, did a cursory glance around to make sure nothing looked too disgraceful, set up some silverware and plates by the coffee table, switched on a light...then chugged upstairs for a shower himself.

She made it downstairs before he did. As he'd guessed, his T-shirt could have fit two of her, and maybe she was wearing her nylon shorts, maybe not...who could tell, with his shirt flopping midthigh on her? She was all legs and hair, and he liked the whole picture, her smelling of his soaps and shampoo, her using his brush, her bare feet in his place.

By the time he'd served lasagna on the coffee table, she'd taken his advice to wander around the place.

"Beer, wine, water, sweet tea?"

"Whatever you're drinking would be great."

He opted for two huge glasses of sweet tea, and by the time they were hunched over the coffee table, the conversation was naturally easy. "The picture over there..." she began, motioning to the rough-hewn bookcases, every shelf filled, hodgepodge, with books and games and films and pictures and what all. Naturally she'd homed in on the one photo.

"Yeah. My ex-wife." He pulled a wedge of hot bread,

handed it to her. "Will wanted a picture of his mom around. He picked that one. Awful, isn't it?"

She looked startled. "Tucker! She's beautiful!"

"I guess. I just think that picture looks a little too much like her. Angie's got her perfect face on. Like her face would crack if she smiled any harder. Like her hair wouldn't move even if she was in a tornado."

She started to unwillingly laugh. "You're crazy. Her hair's gorgeous."

"It always was. She wore it long. Short. In between. Never mattered. You couldn't touch it. I don't know what she put on it, but it always felt a little like...well, like shellac. Ask me, it's downright scary."

"She has good hair! Some of us would give our life savings for good hair!"

"You think that's a *good* trait?" He looked horrified, which earned a wonderful chuckle from her.

"You're a guy. You don't understand." She finished the lasagna, sank back against the old leather couch cushions. "Tucker, this place is fantastic."

"I think so, too. Built around seventy-five years ago, by my great-grandfather. It was never meant to be a full-time house for anyone. Just meant to be the family lodge, where all the relatives could descend for Thanksgiving and Christmas or during the summer. Or whenever. By the time my parents' generation were grown, though, no one had a love for the place but me—and to a point, my brother and sister."

"Well, everything is just so beautifully thought out." She went through a long list. The giant stone fireplace, midroom, with grates both in the dining area and living room. Verandas wrapping both the main floor and the second story. All six rooms upstairs with doors that opened onto the veranda. Endless spectacular views of the mountains and valley.

The cradle-soft leather couches. The oil paintings in the living area, not fancy, but all misty, magical views of Whisper Mountain. A collection of arrowheads under glass. The terra-cotta tile floors, so easy to care for, so cool in the heat, yet area carpets in earthy colors, thick enough to sleep on.

"And I like the bookshelves."

"They get mighty dusty."

"I didn't notice. I just noticed all the photos, the books. Oh. And I love the double staircase—the three-tiered one from in here, then the circular one from the end of the kitchen. If I were a kid, I could have played hide-and-seek here all day."

"When I was a kid, I did just that. There's a room upstairs with all mirrors—"

"I happened to notice it when I was walking out of the shower—it was just so interesting, a room made for closets, with mirrors on all the closet doors."

"My grandmother loved to sew. That was her fancy sewing room. Now…well, I put shelves in half the closets. Most of the bedrooms, Will and I just close off. I don't need to clean 'em or see them. But there are a ton of sheets and towels, set up for a zillion guests. Garnet…?"

"Hmm?"

"You were a little freaked about getting in the kayak this morning, weren't you?"

She tucked up her bare legs, turned her head. "I was," she admitted. "It was weird. I can swim well. I've been on boats."

"Not that I'd know," he said quietly, "but I'm guessing it was about control. A need to be *in* control. Which you wouldn't be, once you climbed in the kayak."

"Tucker, I'm no control addict—"

"I never meant to imply that. I'm saying…for me, and maybe you feel the same, it's a lot easier for me to take charge. Like if I'm driving. Or building something. Or setting up a plan. Things may not work out. But I still feel safer if I'm the one behind the wheel."

She cocked her head, regarding him quietly. "Yeah. I *am* the same. Like with my vanilla plants—I can't help the weather, can't control whether we have rain or sunshine. But I have to be the one to make the decision about how they're fed, how they're treated, how they're nurtured. If something's screwed up, it's all on me. But I just want to have responsibility over the stuff I can control."

He nodded agreement. "I felt the same way even when I was a kid. I could take a hit or a hurt a whole lot easier if it was my fault, my mistake." He shrugged. "No one can let you down if you're holding all the cards."

She cocked her head. "I think that's partly true. But everyone gets let down sometime, Tucker. Nobody gets an escape card for that every time."

"Yeah. Everyone gets some bumps, some life hurts. But when you're a kid, and the people who are supposed to protect you let you down, I think that kind of hurt festers a lot longer. So you grow up, trying harder to put yourself in a position where others can't hurt you that way."

"Are we still talking about kayaking?" she murmured.

He didn't have a clue what they were talking about. She wanted him. She'd been hungry, and now she was clean and full, and the hours of sun and fun were all helping to lower her defenses. Most of the time, she tried not to look at him directly. But now, when she'd forgotten why she did that, her gaze met his naturally.

Just as naturally as a struck match causing flame.

He loved to look at her. Loved the look of her. And she looked at him the same way, with the same greedy eyes, the same interest in every plane and hollow, every angle of her face, every expression in her eyes, the way her mouth moved. The way the temperature rose in his air-conditioned living room to somewhere past ninety, but who was measuring it?

"Garnet?"

"Hmm."

"I'll answer that question. In two shakes. Let me just grab these few dishes and get 'em out of our way."

"You want my help?"

"Sheesh. No. If it takes three minutes, I'd be gob-smacked." He smiled at her.

She smiled back, one of those real smiles of hers, warm, infectious, earthy. "It's been a *great* day, Tucker. You were brilliant to think of the whole plan."

"I had a great time, too. And you know the boys did." By then he'd stood up, grabbed the two plates and silverware, but somehow he couldn't move toward the kitchen, because she was still smiling at him. Still glowing. Still...

Inviting him.

And he knew exactly what she was inviting.

"I'll be *right* back," he promised, and meant it. He raced to the kitchen, yanked open the dishwasher, threw the dishes in, threw in the silverware, grabbed the left-over pan, stashed it in the fridge, washed his hands, wiped his hands, then galloped back to Garnet.

She wanted him, all right.

She was curled up on the couch, in a pose he could only think of as seductive. Her T-shirt had ridden up, still covered her behind, but only by inches. The neck opening had draped open to reveal part of one shoulder, and that one side of her creamy, soft neck. Her hair was splayed on the pillow like the Lorelei in the old story. Her lips were even parted, as if waiting for his kiss.

Only her eyes were closed.

She'd dropped off like a chunk of lead.

With a sigh, he hunted up a light blanket, came back, draped it around her, clicked off all the lights except a lamp on the hearth. When she woke up, he didn't want her groping in the dark, not knowing where she was.

He had a bad feeling, a bad, bad feeling, that she was so far gone she wouldn't likely wake until morning.

This just wasn't working out the way he'd hoped. At all.

Chapter Eight

The dream wakened her. She was lost somewhere, alone, in the dark, stumbling over unfamiliar, rough terrain. Yet there was a low voice, whispering in her ear, promising, promising, promising that she'd find her way. All she had to do was lift her hand and reach out....

She'd had similar dreams before. Not identical, but the songs always had the same refrain. Invariably she woke up before she could do the reaching-out thing. She'd done plenty of that "reaching out" when she was younger. It landed her in quicksand so deep she'd almost never recovered.

As an adult, she'd finally turned a healthy corner. Surviving—and thriving—took accepting that she was plain vanilla, not a princess. That common sense and grit were the only tools that would take her anywhere, and hoping for a Prince Charming didn't get the job done.

The dream was still with her when she opened her eyes...and for a long moment, she was disoriented. The texture of the leather couch was unfamiliar; the light blanket snuggled to her neck was just as unknown. Her gaze was drawn to a small, glass shaded lamp—the only light in the room, but enough for her eyes to adjust from the darkness of sleep.

The lamp perched on a stone hearth—limestone-white, huge stones, and the grate had a fragrant ash, the distant scent of cherry wood. The books, the hearth, the wide windows...she saw it all in a gulp, yet she really only focused on one thing.

Tucker.

He was sound asleep in an easy chair, bare feet cocked up on a footrest, his face taking on the burnished light from the small lamp. He'd put a cover on her, but not one on himself. He was still wearing the old khaki shorts and the T-shirt he'd put on before dinner, so he had to be chilled.

He didn't look cold. He looked like the ideal hot male, all testosterone and sexy eyes, all those shoulders, no hips, that slow, dangerous smile.

Behind his head, she could see the photograph of his ex-wife, which struck her again as a major good-grief. The woman was a card-carrying beauty, the ideal of a Southern woman—confident, poised, attractive right down to her eyeteeth. Garnet knew even before she'd seen the photo that men were invariably attracted to a type.

Tucker's ex-wife was a vision of a Southern belle, the kind of woman Garnet's mom and sisters were... the kind she'd never be.

Garnet rarely fretted about her external appearance. But women like Tucker's ex-wife—like her own mom and sisters—somehow communicated class and pride in how they moved, how they talked, how they looked.

Garnet was as ordinary as peanut butter and jelly. She just never got that invisible classy gene. Couldn't try to be any different than she was.

Abruptly Tucker opened his eyes. Unlike her, he went from sound asleep to sharply awake in a millisecond. That fast, he was staring straight at her, his gaze inhaling her like a silky sip of water.

He wanted her.

She knew that.

It had taken a while before she really believed he felt that sexual zing for her. Because she didn't trust zings—that they meant anything—and she'd been trying her damnedest to avoid any chance touches, any circumstances where she could slip up and make a major mistake. Until now.

"Hope you weren't startled when you woke up on the couch." His voice was whiskey-rough with sleep, but that look in his eyes was as sharply focused as a falcon's.

"No."

He glanced at his watch, then back at her. "It's two in the morning."

She didn't answer. She felt it. His gaze. He didn't touch her—there was a glass coffee table between the leather couch and his chair. But she could feel the stroke, down her arms, where his eyes studied, down her hip, where the sheet draped the shape of her. Her bare feet. Her tousled hair. Her bare lips. He looked... everywhere.

She felt touched everywhere. By him. Only by him.

But unlike Tucker, she knew that giving in could only end badly.

The desire in his eyes didn't change, but he forced himself to lean forward, kick back the ottoman. "I know. You want to go home."

"I should."

"I know my brother said he'd call before bringing the boys back. But I'm guessing you'd feel uncomfortable if the boys came in and found us, spending the night here. No matter how innocent it might have been."

"For me, that'd be a problem," she agreed again. She pushed back the light blanket, swung her legs to the floor.

"And you're not sure what happened at your shop yesterday. I'm sure your two employees locked up, and everything is fine. But I know exactly how it is, when you're the one responsible for everything. I'd want to go home, too. I understand."

"Uh-huh," she said. She crossed around the coffee table. He'd stood up, had a hand rubbing the back of his neck. The hot, dangerous desire in his eyes had changed to a defeated expression. A door had shut down inside Tucker. His Good Man door. He'd locked that inner place up good and tight.

At least until she ambled straight to him, locked her arms around his neck and leveled a kiss on a mouth that was already opening with surprise.

The arm—the one he'd been using to rub the back of his neck—shot up. Dangled in midair. Then, faster than the speed of sound, found its way around her waist. Ditto for his other arm.

Tucker, she'd always guessed, could move faster than a Kentucky Derby winner when he was motivated. Or maybe he'd held back and held back and held back, until the lid just naturally had to blow.

He took over the kiss, went for aching pressure and total possession, eyes closed in concentration, her whole body electrified by the passion pouring from him. He lifted his head once, surfaced for air, said fast and gruffly, "Are you sure?"

"Yes." It's what she did, who she was. She never made a little mistake. Only the big colossal kind. And if she was determined to ask for heartache, she might as well do it whole-hog.

He started walking her across the room, her going backward, him steering. He steered off her T-shirt first—but she was just as quick to yank off his.

She didn't know his house well, much less in the dark, and when they reached the stairs…well, they nearly killed themselves, kissing when she was a step above him, then when he was a step above her, then almost falling. His low laugh inspired her, got her heart pumping even harder, made her whisper "yes" over and over, until they finally, finally reached the top of the stairs.

The hall was as black as a cave, but suddenly there was carpet beneath their bare feet—thick, scruffy, but silencing all sounds except for his heavy breathing… and hers. He stopped to lean her against the wall, just to pause for a long, lazy kiss. A kiss with tongues and tastes. Yearning expressed in the dark, loneliness, the hunger to connect with someone else. Someone who mattered.

And once that devastating kiss of truth came out…he slipped his palms in the waistband of her nylon shorts. They caught, midthigh, then shimmied to the ground. It was all she had to wear—his T-shirt, and her shorts—

but it wasn't a lack of clothes that made her feel naked. It was him. How he touched her. How he looked at her, even in the dark.

She slipped her hands to the front of his shorts, homed in on the short zipper. Broke free from a lazy, tasty kiss to murmur, "Wow."

Another low, sexy chuckle from him. "He's a little overexuberant. Been on lockdown for quite a while."

"I can see that. At least he certainly seems to be expressing an extraordinary amount of enthusiasm."

He redirected his focus back on her. "Where'd you get that perfect body, Blondie?"

"On sale at Walmart. Afraid I couldn't find any boobs, though."

"Your boobs are beyond perfect. Delectable. Exquisite. Incomparable—"

"You can go on. I hope you do. But I just need a teensy commercial break…. Um, Tucker, do you have protection?"

"Yes, ma'am. I'm sorry. I'd rather be a reckless, wild daredevil for you…but I'm afraid I've got some kind of genetic Boy Scout in me."

"That's okay. Any minute now I'm going to turn shy and hypernervous. Then you'll be stuck seeing the real me."

"Shy and hypernervous, huh?"

"I'm just trying to tell you the whole truth, so you won't be able to say that I didn't warn you."

"Tell me some more," he said, but he didn't mean it. She was out of conversation, too. They'd crossed a threshold.

He used a foot to close the door, freed a hand to reach behind and lock it. She got it: even if the boys somehow came home in the middle of the night, they wouldn't find their parents in a compromising position. Knowing that, knowing he cared enough to protect the boys…well, it just wasn't fair. A woman could fall in love with a man like that. A man who didn't have to think to put a child first, didn't have to discuss doing the right thing, just did what was right.

"Whoa," he murmured. "Let me catch up."

No. She wasn't giving him any more chances to stop and think. There was no lamplight, but she knew they were in his bedroom. A three-quarter moon was just outside the curtainless French doors. There were shadows, smells, textures, all defining his domain. She glimpsed the light from a doorway—a bathroom beyond. But unlike her place, where clutter reproduced when the lights were off, Tucker was tidy. It was a straight, clean path to the old-fashioned four-poster. Especially if you were in a hurry.

Which she was.

This was different than she'd known. *He* was different than anyone she'd known. The sweep of passion carried her into touches, strokes, caresses that were new to her. He was so rich, her Tucker, so rich in warmth and need and strength.

This wasn't just good. The heat, the need, the honesty, the thrill—this was more than anything, more than everything, wrapped up in how he touched her, how he smiled in the dark…just before he pounced for another kiss, another little bite. He flipped her over as if she were cotton fluff, tongued the whole length of her spine…slowly. Then flipped her back and knelt between her legs. And went slowly. Slower than torture, slower than satin, he dipped his head down, took a lazy, luxurious taste of her, lifted his head with a grin.

"That's it," she said, and quit messing around. It was time to show the man who was boss.

She climbed on. Tummy to tummy, breast to chest, rubbing all of her against all of him, nestling her mouth in the hollow of his throat, under his chin…and that was all she could take of playing, even her way. She reared up, straddled him, bent forward so she could frame his face in her hands.

"Hey, Tucker," she whispered.

"Yup, it's me."

"We going to do this fast or slow?"

"Yes."

"Are we going to take turns or just elect a boss for this time?"

"Yes."

"You want to rest, maybe discuss politics or the weather for a little break?"

"You are *not* a good woman. I don't care what I told you before," he hissed, and even though he was beneath her, just like that, he surged inside of her.

The sensation of being filled, so completely, took her breath. She heard a yelp escape her throat, his coaxing murmur, and then his big hands framed her hips, started a rhythm. She knew the music, his music, the crescendo and drum rolls and heartbeat that sent her blood heating, racing. With him. The whole rock-and-roll ride was with him. Eyes open. Eyes blurry with emotion.

Need sharpened inside her. It hurt. Ached like fire. She needed…

Needed.

Him.

The crest-over stunned her. He let out a growl of a cry, and then just wrapped his long strong arms around her…both of them too spent to talk. Too spent to think.

And for her, too filled with an impossible sense of joy and wonder.

"You have to drive me home."

Tucker turned his head. "I know. Don't worry. I'll get you home before daybreak, I promise."

"Hey!"

"Hey what?"

"That was another kiss!"

"I'm trying to give myself motivation to move. Otherwise I'm almost sure I'll never find the strength to get up and drive you home," he said, defending himself.

"Tucker. You're bad to the bone."

He wasn't. It was all her, inspiring him to be bad. All he had to do was kiss her—a serious kiss—and she was winding around him again, doing that Lorelei rub, breast to chest, her pelvis rocking against his. She was extraordinarily passionate. Extraordinarily responsive. Extraordinary at shaking his timbers.

"You could say no," he reminded her.

"So could you!"

"You could say you were tired or that you'd had enough."

"So could you."

So it was Round Three. This time, he tried a slow waltz instead of a fast rock and roll. This time he really wanted to savor, to take precious care, to respect every inch of her. This time…he really wanted to hear her moan. Now that was music.

After that…well, he was more tired than a zombie. So was she. But under the circumstances, they both aimed for a shower, and ended up in the shower together, and in spite of impossible odds—for him—he somehow threw insanity to the winds and went for a fourth time.

They were both giddy as kids, making silly comments, laughing at jokes that weren't jokes, when they finally pulled on serious clothes and aimed for the truck. He really did need to drive her home before sunup... only the ride proved to be unexpectedly startling. The mountain road was asphalt, shiny with dew, trees glistening shadows, whispers coming off the mountain.

He was starting to believe in those whispers.

Which unfortunately made him want to talk about it. "Garnet...for me, this night changed everything."

She turned her head, but in the darkness of the cab, he couldn't see her expression. "In what way?"

"For a long time, I'd been hoping...that we'd find ourselves together. In more ways than just being parents of sons the same age. But I never expected everything that happened tonight. Everything that you were. Everything that we were together."

"You don't have to say that, Tucker."

The road was too sharp, too challenging in the dark, to turn and look at her. So he couldn't see her frown, but he sensed it. "I was hoping you felt the same way."

She didn't immediately respond. The silence only lasted a millisecond, but a millisecond was too long just then. A couple of thudding heartbeats later she started a gentle monologue.

"I felt more than the same way, Tucker. I never expected to feel anything...the way you made me feel tonight."

That was good, he thought. So damned if he knew why his pulse was still thudding.

"I didn't know. That it could be so different, making love with a man. I only knew Johnny, and he was a boy. I thought the sun rose and set with him at the time. And in that second and a half, I got pregnant, and we got married, and my world pretty much turned into an avalanche."

Her voice was as soft as butter, yet he kept getting that itchy feeling—like waiting for a dentist or a tetanus shot or someone to punch him in the gut—that something was seriously wrong. Not right. He'd been so sure that everything was right between them.

"It took me a long time," she said honestly, "to figure things out. When Johnny died overseas...well, we'd never had a chance to talk things through. He never wanted to be married, not to me. So when he died... it really weighed on my heart. I didn't feel responsible, exactly. In high school, he and I were both dumb as rocks. We both tried to do the right thing about the pregnancy...but truthfully, we did everything wrong. He was a runner. I can't blame myself for that. But it hurt—that he'd rather risk danger, risk his life, go thousands of miles away, rather than even try making a life with me."

"Hey." He'd tried not to interrupt, but there was a limit. He wasn't going to call her Johnny a turnip. At some point she must have loved him. But a guy who'd go off and leave a young woman with a baby was less than a turnip. And a guy who'd make her feel that unwanted was lower than pond sludge. "Why he chose to go overseas, I don't know. To me, it was the wrong thing to do. But right or wrong—it's on him. Not on you."

She nodded, but she was facing front. "Maybe so. But here's the thing. Once I was alone...I started building a life. A real life. Not just for Pete, but with Pete. A life I could be proud of, a life I am proud of."

"As you sure as hell should be."

"Thanks. But I wasn't looking for an atta-girl or a compliment, Tucker. I was trying to say...tonight had no strings. I'm really happy we had these hours together. They were beyond wonderful for me. But I would never make an assumption that sex is binding, or that making love automatically forces us to put a label on our relationship. The truth is, in my life, in my heart, I seem to do best alone."

"Garnet..." He pulled into her drive.

"Hmm?"

"When you're talking to me, you have to try dumbing it down. I'm not real good with subtle messages. And I don't have a clue what you're trying to tell me."

"Yes, you do," she said gently. "We're not headed for the altar or long-term. I knew that going in. And it's okay. I'm just totally glad for what we had tonight."

She leaned over, smacked his cheek and then jumped out of his truck and skedaddled to her house. He wanted to go after her. Wanted to...shake her or something. They'd discovered a connection tonight like he'd never experienced before. She'd sure communicated under the sheets that she'd experienced the same rare connection.

Yet now she was pushing him away. It didn't make sense...except that he'd specifically been afraid of this. That Garnet didn't want long-term with him, didn't want the blended family of double sons they'd have together.

He didn't know why. Needed to know why. But there was no going after her to clear this up. The damned sun was peeking over the horizon. The boys could be coming home to his place any second.

All week, Garnet had been so crabby that her employees were threatening to fire her. Mary Lou claimed she was jumpier than a cat in the rain. Sally repeatedly told her to just go, git, go shopping or put her feet up or do whatever she wanted—except be underfoot in the shop. She couldn't sleep. Wasn't hungry. Couldn't think.

She'd never been moody. Ever.

Until the night she'd made love with Tucker.

Abruptly she noticed his truck pulling in. It was a trade-boys day. Pete couldn't wait to gallop toward Tucker, and Will bounded from Tucker's truck with the same enthusiasm. It was one of those days—the sun scalding down at nearly a hundred degrees, no breeze in sight or sound. She had a thousand things to do, but it was too hot to do any of them.

Will streaked toward her like an energetic puppy. Impossible not to smile at him, although her eyes tracked Tucker as the white truck backed out of the drive. She could see he was talking to Petie, knew perfectly well there'd been no chance of a private conversation since the night they'd made love. Conversations with the boys present was easy enough—but trying to talk without the boys or work interrupting had just been impossible. She just kept feeling more and more uneasy...about what that night meant to him.

About what that night meant to her.

"It's a vanilla day, isn't it?" Will asked, but he already knew, judging from the way he was trotting straight toward the vanilla house. It was Will's favorite thing, possibly because the only ones who worked in there were she and Will. Originally she'd thought sharing the secret with him would create a bond. Which it had.

Today, though, she wasn't really fit company for man or beast.

"Man, it's hot in here," Will said conversationally.

"I know. Have to remember to keep hydrating— there's always water and Gatorade kept in the small fridge here." She watched him put on gloves—as she did. Their hands didn't need protection, but the plants did—from exposure to disease or insects or external factors that could hurt them. "You know," she said, "I noticed you and Pete talking when your dad's truck pulled up."

"Yeah." Will's gaze skidded from hers.

"I noticed the same thing when I dropped Pete off last Tuesday. That you and he had some things to say that looked private. Because you hustled away from your dad and me."

"Yeah," Will agreed again. Then changed the subject at the speed of light. "You know my Aunt Rosemary, and how she studies wild orchids? She shows me pictures sometimes. And none of those flowers look anything like your vanilla."

"Well, plants aren't defined as orchids because of their looking similarly. Partly they're defined by how they're pollinated…." She went with the science talk. Like Tucker, she was sure the boys were up to something, but neither of them would talk about it. Even racking her brains, she couldn't imagine the pair of them brewing up anything harmful.

"Yeah, I know how they're endangered plants and all," Will agreed.

"And like we talked about before, even though vanilla is in the orchid family…vanilla is the only orchid, at least that I know of, that produces edible fruit. Also, there are well over a hundred types of vanilla vine—but only a couple of those that can be used to make products from vanilla."

"When I have science next year, can I use some of the stuff you tell me?"

"Sure." She was the only one who pruned or touched the plants, but Will had learned to use the irrigation setup—to check for leaks, check the temperature and moisture level in the soil, start the lines.

"I wouldn't have to even look it up. I could just come here. And ask you."

"I think looking up stuff is a good thing. But learning by talking to people or seeing for yourself is a good thing, too, don't you think?"

"And it's a *lot* easier than having to study. When you tell me something, it's interesting. So…what's the next thing we need to do?"

"Don't you want a break? Some water? Cookies?"

"Nah. I'm tough."

Will was a darling. Even if he never stopped talking. But sometimes looking at him was a study in his father. Will was honest to a fault. A doer, not a sitter. He was interested in everything, the kind of kid who dove right in and gave 100 percent.

He was even built like his dad, already tall and lean, shoulders already stretching his T-shirt. He had the same cowlick on the left side. The same full-of-the-devil eyes. He even walked with the same lanky stride.

Still…he was very much a boy.

It was the grown-up Tucker on her mind, the memories of their night together slivering into her consciousness, even when she was working. Even when she was talking to customers. Even, like now, when she was sin-hot and itchy and determined to baby every single vanilla vine even if she keeled over from the heat.

"Uh-oh," Will said suddenly.

"What? What's wrong?" She straightened immediately at the tone in Will's voice. She whipped around with the clippers still in her hand. And immediately saw the problem.

Anyone who lived in South Carolina knew what a

copperhead snake looked like. Or they should. Copperheads were never particularly large, and some considered their copper-and-camouflage coloring to be downright beautiful. Not Garnet.

Garnet didn't consider anything in the pit-viper family to be beautiful. A poisonous snake was a poisonous snake.

This one happened to be between her and the locked greenhouse door.

It wasn't young. Year-old copperheads had yellow tails. This one was almost three feet long—which made him about as big as a copperhead got.

Garnet stopped breathing for a moment. And then did what any red-blooded American woman would do.

Screamed her head off.

Chapter Nine

Tucker balanced on a crooked hunk of granite, waiting for the girls to catch up. There were around forty in the group, all between the ages of twelve and fifteen.

The two-mile hike was expected to be a type of meditation walk. Every turn was unique, wildlife everywhere, some views darned spectacular. Of course, there'd been no sign of wildlife from the first footfall. Girls that age only spoke in shrieks, and likely never saw any of the views because they were too busy chattering nonstop with each other. Or complaining.

He figured this was penance. For falling in love with the wrong woman. For not being able to stop thinking about her. For worrying that she'd told him—in a zillion ways—that she was content being alone, not looking for a relationship. She seemed to have no happy memories of family—outside of Petie—so he could understand why she had no reason to be excited about joining into a nuclear blending family like his own.

Asking for more after all the things she'd said…well, it was like volunteering for heartache.

The cell phone in his shirt pocket vibrated. He frowned. He and the staff tended to use walkie-talkies during the workday, because cell phone reception was iffy at best on the mountain. But when he pulled out the phone and recognized the number, he punched it on immediately.

"Hey, Dad, are you busy?"

"Just doing a hike. About forty kids, halfway through. What's up?"

"Oh. Nothing. At least nothing you'd have to stop a group for. It wouldn't be easy for you to come right now, huh?"

Tucker frowned again, his paternal instincts on alert now. "I can come in two shakes if you need me. What's going on?"

"Nothing, really. There was just this copperhead. And Garnet doesn't let anybody in the vanilla greenhouse but her and me. So I don't know how the snake got in here, maybe it just likes the heat, you know? Anyway, I got a bucket on it. I figured I'd go find a pitchfork. But I wasn't sure if I should lift the bucket, because the snake was pretty mad, and if it got loose, there's a lot of places for it to hide in here. And then there's the other thing."

"The other thing? There's worse than the copperhead?"

"Well, not exactly. It's just Mrs. G. Normally she's pretty cool, you know? She's no sissy. But I guess she isn't so good around snakes. I told her to sit down, put her head between her knees. You know. Like we talked about when people feel dizzy and stuff. Actually I'm not sure she was dizzy. She was screaming pretty loud for a little bit. I think she could have just run out of breath."

"But she has employees right there, doesn't she?"

"Dad, I told you. She doesn't let anybody in the vanilla house. Except for me. Because she trusts me. And it's all secret, what she does in here."

Tucker wiped a hand over his face. "Okay. This is what I want you to do. Leave the snake under the bucket. Don't touch it. And you get Garnet out of there, lock up the greenhouse so she won't worry, then make her sit down in the shade—preferably at her place. Get her something to drink with sugar. Like lemonade or pop or whatever she's got around. Make her sit."

"Dad, I can't make her do anything. She's the grownup, remember?"

"Try." Tucker squinted. "I'll get there. It'll take a little more than two shakes. I'll have to get a couple staff members up here, get them organized, pick up Petie from the office. So know I'm coming—but still, call me again if the snake gets loose or Garnet gets sick or something worse happens, okay?"

"Yeah, okay. 'Bye, Dad."

It was darned hot to have to move mountains, but Tucker put it in high gear, shifted personnel so he could bring his best summer staff to take over the hike—there were other groups on the mountain, but not many counselors who could handle girls this age and survive it. Still, picking up Petie was harder than rearranging schedules affecting more than four hundred people.

"I'm right in the middle of the website rebuild, Mr. Tucker. I can't leave right now."

It was cool and quiet in the office, and the darn kid looked more like an adult than he did. Tucker's desk was clean. The trash bin wasn't overflowing. The usual messages were displayed with thumb tacks on the cork board—naturally, in timed order, and then alphabetized.

"Pete, it's about your mom and a snake. The website can wait."

"Trust me. I can't help her with a snake. So I might as well just stay here and do this."

"Pete, if I have to drive there once, it just makes the most sense for you to come with me."

"But I could stay here. And Will could stay there. We already talked about it. We're okay with it."

"What do you mean, you two *talked* about it? You talked about *what?*"

Pete's cheeks suddenly bloomed rash-red. "I dunno. I was just mumbling."

It came out on the ride down the mountain. Tucker considered himself occasionally gifted at pulling needles out of haystacks, but finally Pete hunched over by the window and started talking.

"The thing is, Will loves his mom. But he said he likes my mom better than he likes *his* mom. Which seems obvious to me, because my mom is pretty awesome. As moms go. She loses stuff *all* the time and sometimes forgets to pay bills. She threw a cup against the wall the last time my grandma gave her a hard time. It broke."

"TMI," Tucker said firmly.

"But Mr. Tucker, you asked. So I'm just trying to explain."

"I wasn't asking about your mother's private business. I was asking what you and Will talked about."

"Oh, yeah. That. Well, I told Will, I hear the women in the shop always trying to talk Mom into going out. You know. Like for an evening. Like a date or something. And she says to Sally, 'I will, I will,' but she never does. I don't remember my dad very well."

"I'm sorry about that."

"Truth is, I don't remember him at all. I think I do. When I look at a picture of him in a uniform, the one that's in my room. Then I think I've seen him looking like that. But I'm not sure if I'm imagining it."

"Pete—" Tucker made his voice stern, making Pete give one of those world-weary sighs again.

"I know, I know. You want to hear what Will and I were thinking. We were just talking, you know. Sometimes we call or email each other. Like after the kayak race. How much we liked doing stuff like that. And how maybe it would be a good idea to let you and my mom have a little time together. So Will called his uncle—"

"Ike was in on this?"

"Well, yeah. How else could we have gotten you two together for time by yourselves? We had to have a *reason*. So Will thought up his Uncle Ike, and we both thought up a plan to just spend the night on the mountain—but inside. Not where there are bugs and stuff. Anyways—"

"You and Will get along pretty well, don't you?"

"Yeah. Why wouldn't we?"

"Well…you're pretty different."

"Like, yeah. But Will's okay that I'm smarter than him. And I'm okay that he's more popular than me. Everyone likes Will. I think that's good, though. It doesn't matter to me. I'm okay by myself. I mean, I don't want anyone to hate me, but—"

They were almost to Plain Vanilla. Tucker had to corral the conversation back to the point.

"I'm having a hard time believing that you boys were actually trying to matchmake your mom and me."

"I don't know what *matchmake* means."

"Getting your mom and me together. Like paired up."

Petie gave another of his old-man sighs. "Look, Mr. Tucker. I don't think we should get the cart ahead of the horse. I mean, it's practically taken my whole life to get her to go out with a guy. It's like one thing at a time, you know? Sometimes my mom just has to get used to something before she's okay with it. Like the cat."

"Is the cat inside yet?"

"Yeah. As of two days ago. I'm pretty sure it snuck in for a reason. Like that she's about to have kittens, so she wants to make a nest somewhere safe. Anyway, when I went to the grocery store with my mom, I put some kitty litter in the cart. My mom acted like she didn't see, but she saw. That's how you have to do things with my mom. Go slow. Let her say no a few million times."

Tucker pulled into the yard, turned the key. "That's some serious advice you gave me, Pete. I appreciate it."

"Thanks."

"Now let's go save your mom. Or…how about if you save your mom and I go see about the snake."

"Works for me." Pete was out the truck door in a flash…almost as fast as Will ran out from Garnet's back door, banging the screen in his rush.

"Dad!"

If he wanted to mull over that impossible conversation about Garnet, there was no time or chance. Will was almost beside himself, both with importance and information. His son had to replay what happened with the snake so far, start to finish, from when Garnet spotted it, what he'd done, what she'd done, what happened after that, what happened after *that*…

The immediate thing he had to handle was the snake. He could do it.

He'd done it a zillion times.

He just liked handling snakes like…well, it was hard to imagine anything he disliked more. He wasn't a screaming meanies kind of guy. It was just…their eyes. The way they slithered. Snakes were a high ick factor. And although the reference books claimed copperheads were generally happy to avoid humans, Tucker's experience was that it took very little to piss them off.

He pulled on boots—he always kept an old pair in the truck for situations just like this. This was no job for sandals. And then he told Will, "I don't want you anywhere near this."

"What? How come?! I can help—"

"I know you can, but you and Pete need to do something important. I saw customer cars in front of the shop, so people are in there, and so are her employees. For a couple minutes, we don't want anyone outside, and especially not near the vanilla greenhouse. Your job is to make sure no one comes near until I call for you, okay?"

"Okay." There. The kids had a job. They were now happier.

Tucker wasn't. He edged the door open to Garnet's infamously private vanilla greenhouse, readily saw the tall green bucket upside down right in the walkway. He wanted to look around—pretty damned amazing, what she had going on in there. But he pulled on elbow-length rubber gloves, which were real fun to wear in temperatures this hot, then grabbed a hoe, and then carefully, carefully lifted the bucket.

He was more than ready to spring…braced for anything…certain he'd have one mighty ticked copperhead on his hands. Instead, there was nothing.

The copperhead was somewhere in the greenhouse,

but not under the bucket. Which meant Tucker had a real fun hunt ahead of him. He started swearing, low as a hum, and after locking the damned door so no one could conceivably get in the damned place by accident, he began snake-searching from the west side of the viney jungle. As he looked up, then down, using the hoe, moving slow, he added to his swearing vocabulary, using words he never used, and inventing a few more just because.

"I did *not* faint." Sheesh, she was surrounded by nags. The shop was closed. Sally and Mary Lou had bullied her into the house, then onto the couch, and were still standing like sentinels, hands on their hips. The boys were sitting on the floor, backs against the far wall, playing some kind of game, but both within hearing distance.

No one was leaving her alone. Afraid she might faint again.

"I told you all. I just stumbled a little and happened to fall. I didn't faint. I've never fainted and I'm not about to take up the habit now."

"But you did, Mrs. G. I saw your eyes close," Will corrected her, and then tried to retell the copperhead story again.

They'd each brought her something to drink—for shock, they all said—which meant she had Gatorade, tea, Kool-Aid and a pop, all dripping sweat on the coffee table in front of her. Mary Lou had brought her a blanket. Then Petie brought her an afghan. Even with the air-conditioning on, it was hotter than blazes—she didn't need any covering, but every time she tried to sit up, four sets of hands pushed her back down again.

To add insult to injury, the cat—the damned cat that

wasn't hers—had taken up roost on the red velvet chair in the far corner. The chair and unique table were obviously her treasures. She obviously didn't spend money frivolously. Her whole place was decorated on a dime. She just seemed to need a couple of things that were all hers, even if they were impractical and like nothing else she had. And now the fattest cat this side of the Smokies was purring from across the room, shedding hair on the gorgeous red velvet.

It was almost enough to make her cry.

And then Tucker walked in, like a hurricane blast of testosterone, all sticky-hot and stomping-energy. "It took a while, but the score was finally one for the humans, zero for the snake."

"Did you kill it, Dad? Did you kill it?"

"No. I wanted to. We weren't pals. It was quite a confrontation, and for a while, I wasn't sure who was going to win out. But she's removed from the greenhouse, removed from the property a good three miles from here." He was still talking when he leaned around the cluster of bodies and finally spotted her. His frown was instant. "Hey, what's wrong?"

"Nothing," she said immediately, only the swarm of boys and women immediately told them—all at once— how she'd keeled over and they'd had to watch her ever since because she wasn't listening to anybody.

He parted the seas, loomed closer. He probably couldn't hear over the caterwauling, but it only took three shakes before he'd planted a rough hand against the side of her neck, checking for heartbeat or pulse or temperature or something—who knew?—then removed the blankets and sat her up. The whole time he was looking at her. Not *looking* at her, the way he'd looked at her the night they made love. But just…looking. Like a scientist examining a specimen. Checking for skin color and eyes and sweating and any other annoying signs of illness.

"Okay," he said to the crew. "Here's the deal. Mary Lou and Susan—"

"Sally," her employee corrected him.

"I'm sorry. Sally. I promise you both I'll make sure she's taken care of—including dinner and supervision to make sure she eats something. Does the shop need locking up?"

"No, we did that," Mary Lou said, but she was sending him mistrustful glances. "It's always Garnet who counts the money and sets all that to rights. And that's still in the cash register."

"I'm guessing Pete can be trusted to do that," Tucker said.

"Well, yeah," Pete said, as if that should have been obvious to anyone.

"There are things she wouldn't let strangers do," Mary Lou said sternly, standing like a marine sergeant, arms crossed.

"Then I definitely won't do those things," Tucker said. "But I'm guessing if Garnet's not feeling her best, she could use some quiet and rest, and the faster we all get out of here, the faster that can happen."

Garnet couldn't believe how quickly he cleared the room. Mary Lou sent him a couple more warning glares, but she eventually let out her last "hmph" and aimed for the door. Sally was already there, glancing nervously at her watch—Garnet worried there might be trouble if Sally arrived home even a few minutes late. "Just call him," she urged her quietly.

"Yeah, I will. But you quit fretting about all of us." That was Sally's last parting shot. When she'd become completely surrounded by so many bossy people, she had no idea.

Will and Pete swarmed Tucker, wanting to hear how he'd captured the copperhead, what danger he was in, how scared he was, how menacing the snake was and all that blah blah blah. The makings of bacon and peanut butter sandwiches ensued—apparently Tucker's specialty, the pouring of milk and making of sandwiches—after which, the boys disappeared outside with their paper plates. Tucker finger-clasped the range of glasses on her coffee table, made them disappear and then returned to hunker down on the coffee table with their sandwiches.

Before he'd even said a word, the damn cat stood up, stretched, carefully leaped down from the red velvet chair and waddled over to the two of them. She'd leaped up to the coffee table before Garnet could scold her. Garnet decided she would simply ignore her altogether.

That wasn't hard, when Tucker claimed all of her attention the instant he sat that close.

"Quit looking at me," she said. "I haven't had a chance to brush my hair or wash my face in hours."

"You look breathtaking."

"I wasn't fishing for a compliment."

"Okay, I'm so sorry I said that." He cocked his head. "You're really freaked by snakes, huh?"

"Yes. I admit it. I can do the occasional bear, lots of deer, skunks, mice, I've nursed hawks back to life, and one batch of motherless raccoons—don't ask. Pete made me. I had to. Anyway. Give me anything but snakes. I can't help it. They just give me the willies."

"Lots of snakes in South Carolina."

"Thanks for reminding me of that."

A wry grin. He'd finished his sandwich in about

three seconds. "I'm just saying, you love being outside. I'd think you'd be used to snakes by now."

"That'll happen when it rains money."

"Are we feeling a little testy?"

"I *didn't* faint."

"I believe you."

"I just got a little sick to my stomach. And had to sit down."

"That's pretty much how Will told it. Just a couple details different." He lifted his hands in an innocent expression, just as she was about to brain him with the paper plate. "You're feeling okay? That's all I was trying to ask."

"I'm *fine.* And very sorry you got dragged over here in the middle of your workday."

"You saved me from a couple dozen tweens. All females. I was sinking fast. In fact, when Will called me, I was so grateful, I almost cried—especially when I had such a righteous excuse about needing to save a damsel in distress. So *please, please* call me the next time—anytime—you run across another snake."

Darn man made her grin. And then laugh. "Okay," she admitted finally, "I know I've been a pill. Everyone was…*hovering.*"

"I don't do well with hoverers, either. No need to apologize." He scooped their paper plates and napkins together, set them aside, hunkered closer. "I do need to get home—and to get Will home. But I need to tell you something before I go—and before the boys charge back in."

"What?"

"While we were driving here, Pete told me something." Suddenly he was looking at her again. Not looking, as if examining her for bruises and scars. But looking the way he'd looked the other night. The night they'd made love. The night that kept replaying in her mind like a love song she couldn't stop humming.

"Pete told me that he and Will have had a number of conversations about the two of us. Apparently they've been conspiring, trying to manipulate ways to get the two of us together. Like they called my brother Ike. Ike was set up to drive us to the start of the kayak race— but it was the boys who conned him into the night on the mountain, so that we'd have private time together." He was still looking at her. The same way. The way that made the blood rush to her tender spots, and her lungs suffer from an inability to take in air, and the rest of the room to swim off in some murky distance, while he filled her screen. All of her screen. In surround sound and high definition.

"I kept asking him questions," Tucker said. "It was hard for me to believe the two of them were matchmaking. Hoping we'd hook up."

There, now. Garnet thought she was having trouble breathing before, but now she suffered from complete oxygen failure. It went into her lungs. It just wouldn't go out.

Until that instant, maybe—*maybe*—she hadn't been dead positive she'd fallen heart and soul for Tucker. But hearing him talk about the boys matchmaking, the kids thinking they just might belong together...her heart suddenly clutched, tight as a fist. A soft fist. Maybe, just maybe, in that closed door where her heart used to be, she'd been dreaming they got along amazingly well. That she'd never felt as wonderful as when she was with him. That if fairy tales were just true—even though she didn't believe in happily-ever-afters—she could imagine herself so easily waking up to Tucker. For the rest of her life. And just maybe into the next.

But…there. Her heart stopped hammering and slowed all the way down. He'd brought it up with a smile, like the boys matchmaking was a joke. And that brought a slap of reality like nothing else. She was plain vanilla, how many times did she have to remind herself of that? He was practically South Carolina aristocracy.

And she knew—she *knew*—how prone she was to make dumb, impulsive mistakes, where she got her heart ripped out and only glued back together with cracks.

"That's funny, Tucker," she said with a grin.

"Funny."

He just echoed the word. Not with a question or a sound of an agreement. Just…said it.

Garnet pressed on, certain she could make him comfortable with the situation. "I'm glad you told me. Petie's always beyond imaginative. I hope you weren't embarrassed. Really, I think it's partly a measure that your whole plan is working."

"My…plan."

"Yeah. Your plan. To trade the boys. To have Will find a way to talk easier with females…for Petie to find a way to do more guy things. Easy to see that Pete thinks of you as a father figure. A good guy. A male he can talk to, be honest with. I'm thrilled."

"You're not sounding that thrilled."

"I am. I am. I'm thrilled hugely. I just have to laugh a little. That the boys would think up anything quite that preposterous. I hope your brother wasn't weirded out by the whole thing."

"Preposterous. Our getting together. That's how you'd see it?"

"Of course." She smiled. Her biggest, bestest, brightest smile.

And then, of all things, he leaned over, swore—even said the really bad thing—and then slammed her head back into the couch with a kiss. A lip-crushing, mouth-sealing, hot-blooded kiss. Tongues and teeth got involved. Her body went limp from the waist down. Her eyes even closed. It was all she could handle, just taking in the whole of that kiss…take it in, his taste, his scent, all of him….

A few hours later—or maybe a few seconds—he lifted his head. Scowled darkly at her. Said, "I'm tracking down Will. We'll be out of here."

"Okay, I…" She had to suck in a breath. "Tucker—"

"Don't say *anything* to me right now. Not one thing."

"You're mad? At me?"

He never answered. He just slammed the screen door on his way out.

She put her hands on her hips, not sure whether she felt more mystified or more upset. She'd been trying to reassure him, not trouble him. And his anger seemed a measure that she'd let him down in some way—but she didn't know how.

And then she realized, she'd never thanked him about the snake. For being her hero, and leaving his own responsibilities to take care of hers.

When Tucker pulled up two days later, he still hadn't shaken his ticked-off mood. Pete and Will did their running past each other, high-fiving in the middle of the driveway. Will hadn't seemed to notice his ornery moods, and Pete popped into the truck, with a sunshine-big grin and his arms loaded.

"Hey, Mr. T. My mom made you a strawberry rhubarb pie, to say thanks for taking care of the snake. Oh, and there's a batch of cookies in the other tin. Cherry chocolate chip. You don't have to share them. They're all for you. But just so you know, her cherry chocolate chip are the best in the world, even if she's not so good at cooking other stuff."

Pies. Cookies.

His favorite pie, not that she could have known that.

Petie's favorite cookie, which she obviously knew.

But nothing hinting that making love had changed anything for her. They were single-parenting buddies. That was all she seemed to want.

Sex was always a game changer for a woman. Except Garnet. Guys weren't supposed to fall so fast. Only Tucker *had* fallen. High and dry.

Making love with her had sealed what he'd already known—that she was special. Unique. They fit together the way no woman had ever fit so perfectly for him and with him.

"My mom said that she and Will cooked up another team challenge. It's a burger contest. Like who makes the best burger. Like on the day after the Fourth of July, if you can." Pete switched the truck radio from country to rock. "This'll be an easy win for us. My mom can't cook worth beans. Come to think of it, she can't cook beans, either."

When Pete kept looking at him, as if waiting for an answer, Tucker said, "Sure. That sounds fine."

"Mr. T., I have a question for you." Clearly switching gears, Pete used his most earnest voice. Tucker had heard it before.

"Yeah, you can have a look at my accounting program. But you can't make changes. Or do anything else, unless you can make it clear to me what you're doing."

"Okay, but that wasn't my question."

"Yeah, you can use the Excel program to set up a graph for the challenge course."

"Okay, but you already told me that. In fact, I already started that because I knew you'd say yes. That wasn't my question."

"I give. What's the question?"

"I don't know how busy you are today. But I was wondering, before I go home, if maybe I could have, like, a half hour with you. *Outside*. To do something outside, like you're always pushing me to do."

Tucker shot the kid a quick, suspicious glance. There was so much virtue in Pete's innocent eyes that Tucker could smell that he was being suckered.

"I can't guarantee the free time. You've been around the camp. You know emergencies come up sometimes. But I'll try. What is it you want to do in that half hour?"

"It's about my mom. I was reading about this area—this mountain, your mountain. And years ago there was gold found in the creeks. And garnets. It was a long time ago. But the quartz you have around here, it's still the same type of stone, the same geology, that should still have garnets. And my mom's name is Garnet."

"I know that."

"So I was thinking, we could pan for garnets. In one of the creeks. Just see, you know? If we could come up for a stone for her. And then I could give it to her on her birthday. Which is like three weeks away."

The idea came out of the blue for Tucker. But he thought about it. Particularly since he had yet to find a way to get Petie outside, except for their one kayak adventure. "You know, it wouldn't look like a garnet if it was just rough rock from the stream."

"I know. I saw it in pictures. But that's kind of why

I thought my mom would like it. She doesn't wear a lot of jewelry. She doesn't spend money on stuff like that. But she puts rocks and stones in the kitchen window sometimes. She really likes stuff like that. Things that are, like, natural. My grandma gives her jewelry a lot. She just puts it away someplace. But a stone that's her name...don't you think it's a good idea?"

"Yeah. I think it's a great idea. And you're a good kid to think of it." Tucker shook off his crabby mood. Will was thriving under Garnet's care. He wanted and needed to be as helpful to Pete.

The afternoon was another heat buster, over a hundred degrees, a group of businessmen spending three days on the mountain. A once-outstanding management team had been beaten up over the economy. They showed up two days before, discouraged and grim...but then, off came the suits. Tucker had a time-honored set of team-building exercises, all of them involving dirt, mud and, usually, a whole lot of laughter. The exercises were, of course, booby-trapped in a fashion that no one was a loser and the whole group won, but sometimes that took some finagling. Even some diplomacy.

Tucker had diplomacy when it was ninety degrees. Past a hundred, he tended to run a little short.

When he headed for the office around three-thirty, his throat was parched; his clothes were sticking to him, and he had some solid break time coming. That was, until he stomped in and saw Pete, who popped up from the desk with a hopeful expression.

Tucker gulped. "No, I didn't forget." Sometimes, a guy had to lie. "I just really got tied up with the last group. It's really hot out there. You sure you want to go?"

"I'm sure. I'm even *positive*."

"Okay, okay. I'll get some gear together. You hit the cafeteria, rustle us up three or four bottles of water. I'll get some pans. And a colander..." He was thinking as he moved. "We'll take the Gator. Grab some towels. Maybe a shovel..."

Tucker had no plan to have any fun, but damn. It only took a few minutes before they both started having a blast. The creek bubbled and chased around rocks, with overhanging pines and rhododendron shading the banks from the excessive heat. Neither had brought water shoes, so both peeled down to bare feet.

Tucker shoveled a heap of soil and rock from midstream, poured it in Petie's pan, then used the colander to sift through their treasure water. Minnows tickled their toes, and both saw the occasional silver flash of a bigger fish.

Pete, being Pete, had to give him a lesson as if he were the elder and Tucker was the kid. "Almandite's the name of what we're looking for. It's a mineral. A common mineral, even. Found in metamorphic rocks, like schist and gneiss. That's why it could be in this stream. It's all metamorphic rocks around here. And there's lots of quartz and magnetite around here, too. I read there were garnets as big as three feet long from this area."

"Um, Pete? I wouldn't count on us finding a three-foot garnet."

"I'm not *counting* on it. I'm just saying. This is the right mountain for it. And nobody's probably looked for a long time. So that has to make our chances better, don't you think? Isn't this *great?*"

When Pete laughed, Tucker had to gulp. He'd happily walk a mile for one of those laughs. Pete was easy-tempered, but normally so darned serious. A few splashes and slips, though, and he was as soaking wet as Tucker was. No possible harm. They were both cooled off…and what male ever born didn't like to get his hands into mud and rocks?

"And they're not always red, you know. Garnets can be green. Or yellow. Or pink. I'd like a red one for my mom, though."

By then they'd collected a bowl full of potential jewels. Tucker suspected when their loot dried off, it wouldn't add up to more than plain old stones…but that was another so-what. Pete was out, getting fresh air, having a blast, just being a kid.

"Okay. That last batch just had nothing to it. I'm going to wade in another foot or so."

"I have to get out for a second. I'm just going behind a tree."

"No sweat." Everybody had a call of nature now and then. Tucker kept an eye out, to make sure Pete didn't wander too far, but it was only moments later before he galloped back, obviously not willing to miss a second of their garnet hunt. For a few moments, though, he didn't say anything…and when Petie didn't have anything to say, something was usually wrong.

"You need help over there?" Tucker asked. They were only a few feet apart, both scrunched on slippery cool rocks, wading in the rushing creek up to their knees.

"No, I'm okay."

"Find anything good in this batch?"

"Not yet." A sigh. An old-man sigh.

Now Tucker paid attention. "Something on your mind?"

"No. Well. Sort of. I've got something I've been worried about. But it's just not something you can usually talk about."

End of conversation. Tucker put down his pan, stood

up then. Figured he'd sit on the same rock Pete was on, see if working closer together might make the conversation easier for the kid.

"Hey," he said. "You know the rules. What gets said on the mountain, stays on the mountain. That's what this great place is about. Being at ease with yourself."

"It's just a weird question I have, you know. It's about size. The size of something. The *normal* size of something."

"Size of what?" Tucker asked. He wasn't just curious now. He was happy Petie felt he could come to him. There wasn't a prayer in the universe he'd let the kid down.

He felt that. Believed that.

Only when Pete suddenly blurted out, "So could you just tell me what the size of your penis is?"

Hell. It was no wonder Tucker lost his footing.

Chapter Ten

Garnet handed a role of purple satin ribbon to Mary Lou. Will was sitting on the counter, right in the middle of things, swinging his legs and shaking his head.

"I just don't get it. Why anybody'd want one of those things."

Those "things" were lavender and rosemary sachets, made fresh in the back room, bundled in small linen sacks, then tied with the ribbon. "They smell great in a drawer or closet," Garnet told him.

"Yeah. I get that. But who cares what a closet smells like? Or a drawer? I mean, who goes around opening drawers and sniffing? What's the point?"

When her cell vibrated, Garnet was laughing right along with Mary Lou—who used to be a card-carrying curmudgeon. Will had changed that. Mary Lou got a charge out of the boy like nothing else.

Garnet glanced at the wall clock before opening the

phone. It was almost four. It was almost time to trade boys, so she was surprised to see her son's name show up on the cell.

"It's okay. I'm all right, Mom," was how Petie started the conversation.

Naturally, Garnet gulped. Those words were inspired to give any mom a major ulcer. "What happened?"

"Nothing. I'm just gonna be a little late. So you shouldn't pick me up for another twenty minutes or so."

"What happened?" Garnet said again, this time feeling alarm climb up her pulse.

"Nothing, really. I mean, nothing bad. Me and Mr. Tucker were out doing something important that I don't want to tell you about. Only he slipped and fell. That's all. He's fine now. He just said I had to call, so you'd know I wasn't at the house by four."

"Are you hurt?"

"No. It wasn't me who fell. It was just Mr. Tucker. And he's okay now. There was just a lot of blood at first."

Okay. Instant heart attack. "Where are you both, right this minute?"

"Up on the mountain. In this secret place. I got him all bandaged up, Mom. I knew what I was doing. It's just getting him back to the house. We're gonna go slow. We drove the Gator here. Mr. Tucker said I couldn't drive it, but I think he might let me if—"

"Peter Andrew Cattrell. You stay right where you are. Will and I are on the way to the van right now. We'll be there as soon as we can."

"Okay. I'm just saying. Don't hurry."

Garnet stared at the phone, disbelieving when her son clicked off. "Will. Grab your stuff. Mary Lou, can you lock up at five? Damn. Where are my keys?"

"Sure," Mary Lou said. "Is Pete all right?"

"He's fine, he's fine." She patted her front shorts pockets. Her back shorts pockets.

Will said, in the same tone of voice her son used, "Mrs. G. The keys are in the van. You always leave them there."

"I knew that."

"Uh-huh."

"Do you know where Pete went with your dad?"

"I didn't know Pete went anywhere with my dad today."

"Do you think my van'll go off-road okay?"

"No. But I can get you wherever they are on one of the Gators."

"No."

"No what?"

"No, you're not driving a Gator. Good try."

"If you're going to drive this fast, you want me to keep a lookout for cops?"

By then, they were, of course, on the road. She sort of spun the wheels getting out of the drive, and possibly took the first set of curves on two wheels.

"I'm going to slow down immediately," she told Will.

"Mrs. G., if my dad were bad hurt, someone would have called me right away."

"Nobody's bad hurt."

"So we're just going this fast for fun, huh?" Will nodded. "I know. You're worried about my dad."

"I'm not worried about anyone."

"Well, you can't be worried about Pete because you already said a bunch of times that he wasn't hurt at all. So that means you have to be worried about my dad. And I think that's nice and all. But I know him really well. Better than anyone else. He's careful. And he doesn't do dumb things. And someone at camp will know where he is, because he always leaves word. And he could have used a walkie-talkie to communicate that he needed help. But he didn't. And he didn't use a cell phone to call me. So those are reasons you could be sure he's okay."

"I'm sure he is."

"It's okay that you like my dad. Pete and I both know you do. Uh-oh."

"I was never going to hit that guardrail, Will." She shot him a baleful glance, and immediately slowed down. Tried to calm down. Tucker had already hinted that the boys had expectations or hopes regarding the two of them. It shouldn't have been a surprise that the comment came out of Will's mouth.

But it was definitely a surprise—and a shock—that Will seemed to realize before she did that she was in love with his dad.

She was.

Hook, line and that whole shebang.

And she had only one instinct if Tucker had been hurt. To get there. Be there for him. Immediately. An hour ago. Before whatever even happened. Which should have given her a teensy clue that he was no friend to her, no comrade, no fellow single parent, but a guy she cared about deeply, instinctively, and straight from the heart.

She zoomed up the drive to Whisper Mountain, paused at Tucker's place, saw that neither the Gator nor the truck were there, and listened to Will's directions on how to get to the office. En route—it wasn't far—she started a careful conversation with Will.

"I have to tell you something," she began.

"What?"

"You're really reassuring and calming in a tense situation. Anyone ever tell you that before?"

"No. Not sure what you mean."

"Well…like just now. And with the snake last week. You're the kind of person—just like your dad—who steps up. Does the right thing."

He turned, as she expected, bright red.

"I'm not trying to embarrass you. Or even to give you a compliment. I just thought you might want to be aware… I'm a strong female, Will. I don't get shaken easily. But some situations push my buttons."

"Like snakes."

"Yeah, exactly like snakes. And I have to tell you, if I'm in trouble or some big problematic situation, you're exactly the kind of guy I'd like to have close by."

"Okay." If he turned any redder, he was likely going to explode. He clearly wanted her to stop talking about him.

"I just want you to know that. To think about it. Maybe you feel you're shy around girls. Or that you don't know what to say around certain females. But every girl doesn't want you to talk nonstop, Will. They're drawn to a guy who makes them feel safe. And comfortable. And you do that just plain naturally. You don't have to think about it or worry about it. It's just part of you."

"There's the office," Will said.

Yeah. She knew he wanted her to shut up. She just figured that was the whole point of their spending time together, for Will to find a way to be comfortable with female people. He needed a comfort zone. A feeling of confidence with female people.

And of course he felt comfortable with her. They dug in the dirt together. Used shovels and water. Discussed bugs. It was no wonder Will'd never felt shy around her. She was probably almost as good as being around a guy.

For the same reason, she'd been pretty positive any feelings Tucker had for her were either propinquity or the ease both genders felt when they could talk to each other without baggage or scars hanging over their heads. He didn't see her as the kind of woman who could hurt him. She was too ordinary to be of importance to him that way.

"Take it easy, Mrs. G. You don't have to run!"

Yeah, well. As much as she wanted to think about Tucker's son, her heart was concentrated on nothing but Tucker. The office was a one-structure affair, with a wide, roofed porch and benches. The door was half-glass, and four open doors could be seen from the entrance—but only one person.

The main room was a mélange of everything—trail and topography maps covered the walls; an aquarium of local spiders sat on a squat table; cases of bottled water stood ready for anyone to take; and one long mural showed Whisper Mountain's array of natural snakes and wildlife.

The man, sitting behind a massive table, was dressed in white canvas, with a netted hat beside him and gloves thick enough for winter. He glanced up when she walked in, smiled at her, but came through with a toothy grin for Will.

"Hey, youngster. How's it hanging?"

"Pretty good, Mr. Willis. This is Mrs. G. Mrs. Cattrell. Pete's mom—"

"I guessed that. I'm Raeburn Willis. Local beekeeper. But I make models for Tucker now and then. Lots of different bees in the woods, different seasons. Knowing how their nests look, where and how they live, that's the best way I know to prevent people from tromping on their territory."

"It's wonderful to meet you, Mr. Willis. I'd love to hear more—it's really interesting—but we need to find Tucker. You know where he is?"

"Shore. He left a note." Raeburn turned a squint on Will. "You know the curve in White Creek, up high, past the stand of hawthorn trees?"

"Oh, yeah. But…" He looked up at Garnet. "I'm going to try the walkie-talkie first. In case they're already on their way, okay?"

It would have been a great idea, if Tucker had only answered—but when he didn't, Garnet's anxiety scaled the stratosphere. No Gators were available for transportation. Will knew the location, but it'd be a tough haul on foot—and then how would they get Tucker home if he was in trouble? Her van wasn't likely to handle the rough-cut paths.

Will kept trying to help. "I just can't think of anything else around. I mean there's a digger. And a brush chopper. And—"

"There's a tractor for brush chopping?"

Will blinked. "You can drive that?"

"Are you kidding? I can drive anything with an engine. Show me where it is."

First she grabbed a backpack with first-aid supplies from the back of the van, and then they were off. It only took two shakes to unhitch the chopper, check the machine for fuel and oil, turn it on. The Massey was relatively new—ten years? A mere child on tractor terms. And a honey, from the way she started up. Obviously there was no extra seating, but she took a look at Will's face, and reached down a hand.

"Climb on. But we're going slow. And if anyone asks, I never let you do this."

"Cross my heart, hope to die," he assured her. "I'll never tell. No matter if someone tortures me. No matter if I had to eat brussels sprouts every day for the rest of my life. No matter—"

"I get the picture. Just come through with the directions, and we have a deal."

The camp roads were all well maintained. The hiking trails were rougher, but no challenge for the tractor. After that, though, they hit snarls and bumps, skinny wedges between pines, rocks that weren't just going to step aside to help them. On foot, they could have made fast time, but the tractor was occasionally like an elephant negotiating narrow halls.

Will kept laughing. "This is really fun, Mrs. G.!"

"If you think we can walk from here—"

"Well, it's another mile or so."

Garnet figured she could find some way to carry Tucker out, if need be. She had a tarp that would work as a stretcher, two boys and herself. And yeah, Petie had told her Tucker was all right...but he'd also said "all that blood." And "all that blood" kept ringing in her ears like the thrum of drums.

She saw a streak of silver just ahead through the brush, cut the tractor engine and immediately heard the creek and birdsong...and voices. Pete's high-pitched tone. Tucker's lower tenor. Felt a heave of a relieved sigh.

Will leaped down first, but she wasn't more than a blink behind.

She hitched the first-aid kit and supplies onto her shoulder, started down a rough scrabble through rhododendron to the creek bank. Stones, all sizes, made a hopscotch path across the creek, and in the middle, on a huge white stone, were the two of them. Tucker and Pete. Laughing.

"*What* are you two doing here?"

Both looked up and saw her. "We can't tell you, Mom," Pete said cheerfully.

Rhododendron plants were busy and thick and scratched at her arms and legs. "And you're laughing. And you're both soaked. Damn it, Tucker. There's blood all over the place!"

"Your son's a fine doc. I'm totally okay. The blood's only because it was a head bump. Heads bleed like crazy. And then your son—that's Mr. Bossy himself—insisted I sit still for a while. Have a snack. He happened to have some Oreos, because your son is always prepared for serious emergencies. Perfect for sugar. That rhubarb pie you sent, by the way, was gone completely about an hour after arrival."

"Good," she snapped.

"If you're feeling sorry for me, you could make another."

She was still negotiating the tangled, steep bank. "I'm *not* feeling sorry for you. I'm ticked at you both. You're both laughing and we were worried half to death."

"I wasn't worried," Will reminded her.

"This is no time to split hairs!"

"Huh? What does that mean?"

"It means, you boys, get together any gear or whatever's around here that needs to go home. I'm going to take a look at Mr. Tucker."

The boys took off faster than buckshot. She unwound her backpack of first-aid supplies and, muttering under her breath, took the first stone step. Immediately, cold, clear water gushed over her sandals, making the next step even more precarious. Tucker didn't say a word—possibly because he was a smarter man than most, possibly because he was afraid. He *should* be good and scared. When she was in a snit, most men, women, children and all wildlife knew to give her a wide berth.

Finally she reached the big flat rock, knelt down and opened her pack to find the hand sterilizer. She rubbed it on her hands as she studied Tucker—but didn't *look* at him. She studied him for injuries, determined not to make eye-to-eye contact. Or any other kind of man-woman contact.

The gash was above his right ear, on the side of his head. She peeled off Petie's handiwork—as far as she could tell her son had done his best to clean the wound, then had unearthed a box of Band-Aids and pretty much used half the box to cover the injury.

The gash wasn't long—an inch or so—but the area around it was swollen and red. It had to hurt like a banshee, but thankfully it was mostly clean, just some fine-grained grit around the edges.

She dug out a bottle of betaine, tore through a sterile wrap to get a large square of gauze. "This shouldn't hurt, but I can't promise," she said. The problem was his hair. The injury was in the middle of it, the sandy color dyed dark red in splotches. She leaned up, closer, pressing against his arm for balance. It wasn't that easy to maneuver on the slick rock, much less while keeping her hands and supplies as sterile as possible.

"I don't think you'll need stitches, but I'm not sure if you'll need a run to the E.R. Where it's grazed, it looks like a raw carpet burn. It's already swelled up. Not as bad as it could be. But definitely not pretty. When we get you back to the house, we'll do ice first. See if we can get the swelling down. Then I think you should try a careful shower, after which we smother the spot with antibiotic cream. Then we relook, decide if we think there's a concussion risk.

"I don't see any sign, but I'm guessing you've had more first-aid training than I have. Not that I'm a slouch at this—I've had all the basic courses. But in your job, I'm sure..."

She turned around, burrowed into her kit again, found a butterfly bandage. By that time she'd lost her place, forgotten what she was talking about. She'd been so busy caring for the head gash that she'd belatedly noticed the scratch just over his eye. Too close to his eye. It looked small, but deep, as if a small, sharp stone had dug in there when he'd fallen. It had to be cleaned and treated and pulled together with the butterfly bandage.

A strand of hair spilled into her eyes; she blew it back, cocked her face so the sun wasn't blazing straight into her eyes, kept studying the scratch. She just wanted to be sure it was absolutely clean before closing it up.

"I don't know what you and Petie were doing. Don't want to know. Don't care. That you got him doing something outdoorsy—you get a medal. And he told you about the dinner idea, didn't he? Will and I versus you and Pete. Who makes the best burger over a fire. What I was thinking was that your son and I—well, we're getting along like a house afire. But it's because I'm like another guy, you know? We play in the dirt. We talk about bugs. We do physical stuff outside. So I'm not really that much of a female influence, which was what this was all supposed to be about.... Hey, buster. Don't move. For two more shakes, okay?"

She didn't wait for him to behave. Just assumed it. And yeah, she could feel the stare of his eyes on hers.

That there were only inches separating their faces, their eyes. Their lips.

But she was paying attention to his sore. Not him.

She was only looking at his sore. Not him.

She botched the first Band-Aid just trying to get it out of the dad-blamed paper. It scrunched and then half of it came off, and her finger touched it, so it wasn't close to sterile. She scrabbled for another.

"The thing is…making dinner is sort of a girl thing. I mean, it shouldn't be. But the point is that, for Will, he's not used to doing girl things. So if we did that together, I thought maybe…well, otherwise, all we've been doing this summer so far is having fun together. I really like your son, you know. Even if he did tattletale about the snake. Now. I think that looks—"

"Garnet?"

"What?"

"You're in love with me."

"I beg your pardon?"

"You're totally. Completely. In love with me."

Her heart suffered failure. Recovered. Thumped hard and fast. "Now where did you get that?" she asked lightly.

"The way you flew here when you thought I was hurt. The way you're taking care of me. The way you're not looking at me. You're not looking at me really hard."

"Well, if that isn't the craziest reasoning I've ever heard," she said crisply. "Let me give you the real picture. I think you haven't been close to a woman in a while. That we've been doing a pretty good job at being friends. We're really good at talking parenting issues together. And then there's chemistry. A couple mountains of it. When you've been celibate for a while—which

I've sure been…and maybe you've been—maybe just about anything could look like love."

"What a bunch of nonsense. Let's go back to the beginning. You're in love with me."

"No."

"Well, damn. I don't like to argue with a woman, but you're forcing me to prove it to you." He leaned up, touched her lips.

Just touched them, yet she suddenly seemed to melt from the inside out. The sky blurred. She heard the rush of water, the whisper of rustling leaves, yet all she really noticed was the luring pull of his mouth, that silk-smooth drugging texture and taste of him.

Her hand shot up to his shoulder—not because she wanted to touch him, but because she would have fallen. The problem seemed to be vertigo. A terrible dizziness. Caused by him.

She sank back down, her rump finding a seat on his thigh. Until that instant, she wasn't aware of straddling his leg—her whole mind had concentrated on getting him bandaged and cared for. But now…her senses seemed on fire. She could feel the grit on her shins, the loamy smell of the creek banks. She could feel heat and wonder and craziness.

Slowly he pulled back. Not far. He looked straight into her eyes, with no smile, his voice as husky as a night wind. "Yeah, Garnet. You're in love with me. And believe it, I feel exactly the same."

She'd have answered him, if she could have just found her voice. He didn't move and she didn't move, and seconds ticked by, moments. Finally she managed to swallow. "Tucker, I'm not hurting anyone else. Especially not you. I've tried my damnedest not to screw up again, but I've got a long record of terrible judgment. You need to believe me."

"I get it. You already sang that song before. You're wrong for me."

"Good boy. You were listening."

"Want to sleep with me tonight?"

"Tucker!"

From the corner of her eye, she saw Will and Pete galloping toward them, carrying heaps of strange things, shovels and pans and what all. She looked straight at Tucker with a scowl, but *now* he'd started smiling. He had the wrong look in his eyes. Anticipation. Intent. A waiting look, like a fox waiting for the henhouse door to open up. He didn't just eat her up with his gaze. He hungered for her. It showed.

And so did the damn man's wicked grin.

"Hey," Pete said. "We're all ready."

Will asked, "What's going on?"

"Nothing," Garnet answered, and tried to scramble off Tucker before the boys noticed anything, but she nearly fell—Tucker hooked an arm around her shoulder to protect her from a tumble.

Both boys stopped sharply, and suddenly exhibited identical bland expressions at finding their parents so close.

She stood up on wobbly legs. "You did a good job with Mr. Tucker's wound," she told Pete in her best business tone.

"Well, yeah. Of course I did."

"But now we need to organize how to get home. Who's going home on the Gator, and who's going on the tractor?"

"You drove the tractor here?" Tucker's eyes shot up in surprise.

"We had to get here. Quickly." She turned toward the boys. "Tucker needs to ride on the Gator for the trek home—it's the smoothest way—so both you boys go with him. I'll drive the tractor back."

"I can drive the tractor—" Tucker started to say.

"No, you won't. The less jostling on that head the better. And I know, I'm not the boss here. But I'm the boss until you're home safe. So don't try arguing with me on this."

"Were we arguing?" Tucker asked the boys.

"I wasn't arguing," Will swore. "Were you arguing?" he asked Pete.

"No. Cross my heart and hope to die. I wasn't arguing," Peter said, and then with a beaming smile for his mother, added, "So you can relax, Mom. No one's arguing."

Relax? The three of them were looking at her like goons. Cloned goons. Letting males of any age vote together was always a mistake.

Damnation if she didn't love them all.

But the eldest... Tucker was becoming a scary problem. She had to figure it out. Who they were together. Who she was with him. Who he was with her. If there was really anything there—besides the hopeless, helpless desire to be with him.

Life wasn't a love song, even if her heart kept crooning that Love-Tucker tune. The kids would be back in school all too soon. Their whole reason to connect would disappear. What they had in common was kids and propinquity. He'd realize soon enough that she wouldn't fit in his life.

She was used to it. She'd never really fit anywhere. She didn't expect to believe her life had suddenly turned into a fairy tale now.

Chapter Eleven

The minute Pete turned off his bedroom light, Garnet sprinted for the bathroom.

They'd gotten Tucker back to his place, had a chance to look at his head under real light and far more sanitary conditions. Then she'd made Will call his uncle, Ike—the one who was a doctor. She'd made food for the group, then hustled Pete home, took care of her business, and finally, finally had a few moments to herself.

In the house, in her life, everywhere, she loved natural, earthy colors...but her bathroom was a downright feminine pink. She flipped on the faucets, stripped down and heaped coconut bath salts into the water. By the time the tub was filled, she'd lit two vanilla candles, poured herself a glass of Shiraz and turned out the light. She took one sip of wine, then slid into the water, leaned her head back against a thick towel and closed her eyes. Okay. She'd had a rattling day, and Tucker had pushed every unsettled button she'd ever had. But she could relax now. She'd shake it off, sleep it off, and face tomorrow—and Tucker—with a clear head.

That thought had just surfaced when her cell buzzed.

Her eyes popped open. She lost her phone several times a day, could probably lose herself in a closet with one door, so why did she have to pick tonight to be responsible with her cell? But there it was, on the pink carpet, next to her robe. She lifted a soaking hand to grab it.

She saw Tucker's name on the screen, and immediately flipped it open.

The complications he'd created for her, with that kiss, with making love, with everything to do with Tucker— none of that mattered. He'd been hurt. Which was of course why she'd kept the phone close. And for the same reason, she didn't waste time on a greeting.

"Your head's killing you? You need me to come and pick up Will, or take you to the doctor? I was hoping your brother was there by now, but—"

"I called Ike and canceled him. My head's fine. It's just a lump. And I'm sorry to call so late, but I was hoping both our boys would be asleep. I needed to talk to you about penises."

"Oh. Of course." She hoped her tone was nonchalant, but she surged up from the water to reach for her glass of wine, took two quick swallows. "I'm so glad you felt you could come to me. Not that I've ever taught sex ed, and frankly, not having that body part myself, I would have assumed you'd know more than me. But I swear, I'll do my best to answer any question—"

He interrupted with a burst of low, throaty laughter. "I *knew* you'd make this fun."

Her heart was so foolhardy. His laughter made her

flush from pleasure from the inside out. "Well, it does seem an unusual topic of conversation for eleven at night, but hey…"

"I can't tell you what I was doing with your son this afternoon, because it's his secret to tell. But while I had him to myself, he came through with a concern he wanted to discuss. His penis. He didn't want to show me how concerned, he just wanted me to tell him what size a 'normal' penis was."

Okay. She supposed she'd have to get serious. "You know, I've tried to talk to him about sexual issues since he was little. Not making a big deal out of it. But trying to respond to things he was seeing in life, or hearing on TV or from kids, whatever. I could have sworn—"

"Garnet, he said he talked to you about 'stuff like that.' This was just different. Because you're female. And I don't think there's a guy born who doesn't start worrying about size starting way before puberty."

She leaned back in the water, relaxing again. "So you think I should talk to him?"

"Nope. I just needed to let you know the conversation happened. It was just a straight-up conversational thing. No weirdness. It's just…I wouldn't want someone talking to my kid without letting me know."

"I appreciate the heads-up." She squeezed her eyes closed. "Oops. I didn't mean to phrase it quite that way."

He'd already let loose another burst of a chuckle. "Two more quick things."

"Are they as interesting as the first subject?"

"Not exactly. The first is that…well, you need to look on the floor in your linen closet."

"Huh?"

"Just when you can."

"Why?"

"Let's just say you'll find something unexpected there. And the last reason I was calling was about our next competition."

"The barbecue. Which team can make the best burger."

"Yes. It's a great idea—but I just need to change a couple of details. Will's mother called. Angie insists she wants him for the ten days starting around the Fourth of July. He doesn't want to go, but she's entitled to that time in the summer, and she claims it's the only space she has."

"That's okay," Garnet assured him. "Things like that have to come first."

"At least by the law they do. At the moment, Will's giving me no end of grief. And the tough part is when he comes back. He'll be a bear. He always is for the first four or five days, until he finally relaxes and turns into my kid again."

Oh, man. She knew what that was like. Her Pete didn't have a second parent in the picture, but when he went to stay with her parents, he came back wound up like a stressed-out top. Still, she didn't offer Tucker empathy. From penises to difficult family issues, they were already on scary ground.

"Anyway," he said, "the point is that I have to change the date of our burger competition. The third Sunday in July is the first day that I don't have groups here—if you could fit in that time."

"I'm okay then." She didn't have a calendar in front of her, and Sundays were busy in the shop, but she knew she could fit it in. Sally, especially, wanted all the hours Garnet could give her.

"Okay. Only one small detail I have to mention about that date. It seems Will told Ike and Rosemary all about our burger grill-off competition. I know you've met them both, but you may not have realized how nosy, intrusive and interfering they are. Which is to say that they called the parents. Now the whole family have elected themselves judges for the burger competition." He cleared his throat, waited. "Garnet? You there? If you don't want to turn this into a family circus, I can call off the extras. Don't worry about it."

"I'm not *worried*." She was just thinking. As soon as he mentioned his family, she had a clutch-up. They weren't old Charleston blood, like her clan, but he came from all those heaps of renowned surgeons and big money and what some in the South called American Royalty under the covers. The kind of people where she invariably didn't fit in.

"I was thinking we could move the contest to my place   and I'd spring for all the grocery expenses, because the extra eaters are on my side. And if that doesn't work for you, it's fine. This has always been about our boys, not outsiders—"

"No, no. It's fine." She gulped. It wouldn't be fine, she was fairly certain. But maybe the change in plans was best. Maybe even perfect. Tucker would see that she didn't fit in. That she was a stranger in that kind of setting. His brother and sister had seemed okay on first meeting, but adding his parents to the mix… She gulped again. "A great idea," she said briskly.

"You're sure?"

"Yup."

"You don't sound so sure."

"I'm sure."

"Where are you?"

"Just watching TV in the living room."

"I'll be darned. I never heard a TV in the background. In fact, I thought I heard the splash of water. You wouldn't be in the tub, would you?"

"Tucker, I'm going to hang up now. You can't just talk about parents and puberty issues and then suddenly just...start trouble."

"So you are in the tub. With the lights off?"

"Tucker! Stop putting pictures in my head!"

"I'm not putting pictures in your head. That's a terribly unfair accusation. I was putting pictures in *my* head. Of you in a nice, deep tub. Hot water. Scented with some great smell. Not flowers. Some other scent. Maybe you lit a couple of candles so you could turn out the lights and really relax. Maybe a beer?"

"Wine," she said, and then stopped herself. "That's it! I mean it! I'm hanging up right this instant!"

"Me, too. But I'll be thinking about you. All night. Leave your window open."

"My window?"

"The mountain. She'll be whispering to you tonight. I guarantee it."

She had to swallow hard before hanging up. Then she flicked the faucet to start draining the tub and stood up in a sloosh of water. She pinched out the candles, grabbed a towel, snapped on the overhead. So much for relaxing. Tucker had made sure that was going to be completely impossible.

She dried off a little, but was too impatient to finish the job, so she just wrapped the thick towel around her and hustled down the hall to the linen closet. The door was supposed to be closed, but since she never remembered to close drawers and doors, it was no surprise to find it slightly ajar. She pulled it open, saw the usual shelves, all the sheets, the towels, the spare blankets, the top shelf of kitchen gadgets her mom kept giving her. No surprises, until she glanced down.

The cat that wasn't hers was curled up on a pale teal blanket, right in the center. She made a sound, not a purr, but more like a welcoming yodel. Four of them. *Four.* Baby kittens were attached to her, and the cat that wasn't hers looked up as if expecting Garnet to share and appreciate her wonder.

Garnet sank to the floor, still holding the towel, and just shook her head. "You think I should be happy for you? Is that your story?"

The cat closed her eyes when Garnet accidentally rubbed between her ears.

"We'll be having the birth control talk before this can happen again," Garnet said sternly. "And you know that was my best blanket. Notice how I used the past tense?"

The cat lifted her chin when Garnet accidentally brushed a thumb under her throat. The kittens looked like rats…but even so, their coloring was downright pretty—silver-gray and white, so unlike their homely mama.

The mama cat reminded her a little of herself…which made her think of her own offspring. She stood up, tied the towel more securely and tiptoed into Petie's room.

He was sleeping in his usual way, knees tucked up, the sheet just so around his neck. Not that she was prejudiced, but he was probably the cutest kid ever born—even when he was being annoying. And the loot Garnet found in his closet was extremely annoying. A water dish. Gourmet cat food. And on the other side of the closet, a litter box.

Oh, yeah. Petie knew about the mama cat, all right. And had to conspire with someone to get those supplies, because he had no way to get to a store by himself. She even suspicioned who would have been his coconspirator. Either of the women who worked for her would do about anything for her son…but they weren't good secret keepers.

It had to be Tucker who'd helped. Tucker who had conspired against her. Tucker who'd gone behind her back.

Dagnabbit. It was hard to ignore the truth when the evidence was all over the place.

She was in love with that man.

But how could she be sure that meant they could make a life together? She just couldn't see how it could possibly end well.

Garnet hadn't seen Will since he'd visited his mother, but when Tucker dropped him off it was the day of their burger competition. She only had to take one look to see what Tucker had been talking about. Will loped into the house with his head down and his expression conveying boredom and gloom. If there were any lights turned on in his upstairs, she sure couldn't see them.

"Did you have a good time in Atlanta with your mom?" she asked.

"Fine."

He'd said "fine" as if it were a four-letter word, so Garnet abruptly changed tactics. "You ready to beat the pants off Pete and your dad?"

"Not really. I don't cook. I never cooked."

"This isn't like cooking, exactly. I have a plan," she said, using Tucker's famous words in Tucker's conspirator tone of voice. "First, we take scissors outside…"

He trudged outside. He held the basket she asked him to. She circled the raised garden beds, ducked under shade slats, wandered under the full sun, snipping a variety of herbs, explaining what each one was, and how they were going to make their burgers differently than anything Pete and his dad could conceivably come up with.

Will responded when she asked a question. Otherwise, it'd take a stethoscope to find out if his heart was beating. The animated, high-energy kid she'd come to know was looking around, staring at clouds, shuffling his feet, connecting with nothing—and for sure, not with her. He didn't want to do anything. Didn't want to talk. His head was slumped so low he walked into things, knocked things over. The more graceless he was, the more bumbling he got.

"You know," she said, "the next part of making our secret burgers is going to take you. I can't do it. I need some brawn. Your kind of brawn. But first… You haven't been here in a while. We had sort of a catastrophe happen around here."

He didn't ask what, just followed her. She set the basket of herbs in the kitchen, took him down the east hall to the linen closet outside Petie's room, sighed—heavily and loudly—and then opened the door.

He took one look, and the sullen expression disappeared. "Oh, my God, oh, my God," he said, and then, stricken, added, "Don't tell my dad I said 'oh, my God,' okay?"

She made the old-as-time gesture of zipping her mouth closed and watched Will drop to the floor with a thud, and that was the end of the bad mood.

The kittens weren't a full three weeks old yet—not old enough to be true hellions. But they'd opened their eyes, and their claws were sharper than tiny razors, and they were starting to get curious.

"When they're nursing like this, you don't want to

pull them away from her," she told Will. "But if you pet the mama first, then touch each of the kittens equally... she'll be fine with your being here. She just needs to trust that you'll be gentle."

"I'll be way gentle. I'll be awesome gentle. I'll be perfect gentle."

"I never doubted that for a minute." She crouched next to him for a few minutes, thinking he'd get tired of the kittens after a while.

He didn't. He looked clearly prepared to camp on the floor indefinitely.

And her floor was distinctly dusty.

She waited. Then waited some more. Then she thought about payback for all the bad, bad things Tucker had done to her. "We need to start on our burger prep, Will."

"It can wait a while, can't it?"

They'd already waited a good while. "Here's the thing," she said gently. "You're going to have *lots* of time with the kittens pretty soon."

"But we're going to my house in a few minutes."

"I know that. But it won't be long before their mom weans them, and then, if you wanted, I was going to give you a couple."

"*Me?* You were going to give me two kittens? You mean, I can have two kittens?!" Will looked at her with abject adoration.

"Oh, yes. I think you'll make a perfect caretaker. You're responsible. And you're respectful. I can't think of a single good reason why your dad would say no." But she subtly tried to corral him toward the kitchen again.

"Right now, though, we need to make those burgers. In fact, when we win the competition, I think it'd be a great time to mention the kittens to your dad."

"You're smart, Mrs. G."

"You are, too. We both know how to outwit parents sometimes, don't we?"

"Yeah." He trudged after her into the kitchen, only tripping once—on a piece of air—and knocking down nothing more breakable than a stack of napkins. "What's the mama cat's name?"

"She has no name."

"But she's yours."

"Well, that seems to be what she's decided. I think that's what cats do. Pick the people they want to love. And if you respect that, they'll likely love you heaps."

"You're sure Pete won't mind if you give me a couple?"

"I wouldn't have made that kind of decision without Pete. He knows we can't keep the kittens. He'll likely be extra glad if you can take a couple, so he'll have a chance to see them now and then." She brought out bowls, then the ground round, then assembled the rest of the ingredients. "Now…I need you to wash your hands really good. No dirt under the fingernails. No forgotten spots. Because I need you to knead all the ingredients together into the meat. It's a messy, icky job, but—"

"Hey. It's okay. I like messy, icky jobs."

"Really?"

"Really," he assured her.

By the time they pulled into Tucker's drive two hours later, Garnet's upbeat mood had taken a complete nosedive. There was no chance of this barbecue competition working out. None. For once the temperature was below ninety, but a hot, testy wind shrieked off the mountain, beating up branches and hissing around corners. She parked behind several other vehicles—one SUV, one brand-new town car, one dirt-crusted Jeep. She stepped out only to have the wind slap her face like a burn, her reasonably tidy hair whipped into a froth. The plan was for Will to help her carry the coolers from the back, but that intent fell by the wayside when Petie charged out of the house, yelling to Will, "Me and your dad are going to whip you guys' butts!"

"Oh, yeah. So you think." More bodies showed up in the doorway. "*Dad!* I thought cooking was for *girls!* Instead it was so fun! Even though I can't tell you what we did to our burgers because it's a secret. And we've got another secret besides that one. Grandma! Grandpa! *Hi!*"

Garnet braced. The stampede out the front door was boisterous and noisy, the sounds distinctive to a loving, connected family who enjoyed being together. Thankfully she already knew Ike and Rosemary. Her gaze homed in on Tucker, but beyond his "About *time* you got here!" she was too swallowed by the group to get near him.

His parents were the surprise. She'd hugely worried about meeting them, partly because Tucker's face and voice always changed when he mentioned his mom and dad. Instead, they weren't remotely terrorizing. Walker McKinnon looked like an older version of Tucker—he was ultra tall, with the same keen eyes and gentle tenor. He greeted her with an affectionate hug, and insisted she call him Walker.

Tucker's mom, June, was just as warm. She wore a MacKinnon Breakaway T-shirt and shorts, and had glossy cinnamon hair and her son's extraordinary blue eyes. She charged over to introduce herself, and immediately won fifty million brownie points by commenting on how smart and interesting and well-mannered Petie was.

Garnet kept trying to zigzag over to Tucker, but the rest of the group kept engaging her in conversations. The whole MacKinnon clan had a surfeit of energy, never stopped talking and laughing—and the grandparents doted on the kids, her Pete getting as much attention as their Will. They didn't ask the same old how-are-you, what-grade-are-you-in, but instead steered conversation toward the kids' interests. June asked Petie to change the ring on her cell phone, as if she couldn't do it herself. Walker engaged Will in a hair-raising golf-cart run—where Will was allowed to drive, to his joy and his father's consternation.

Ike and Tucker were still in the process of setting up two separate barbecues—the goal being to locate them back-to-back, so the competing chefs were facing each other. Garnet had no idea how they were going to grill anything in this crazy wind, but she joined with the women on setting up picnic tables. Rosemary carted out pitchers of lemonade and iced tea. Garnet hustled to empty her coolers, starting with a massive bowl of fresh fruit and trays of garnishes.

Finally, the contest was announced—with some fancy fanfare. The boys produced two trays of burgers, one with a red flag, one with a blue one. Tucker and Pete were given royal blue aprons to don, while Garnet and Will opted for red. Everyone else had bright yellow name tags with JUDGE spelled in capital letters. Rosemary came through with red and blue spatulas for the chefs. Grandpa MacKinnon, alias Walker, blew a whistle.

The judges settled at a long picnic table, cheering and egging on the competitors. The boys held the platter of meat. Tucker and Garnet took up stations behind their respective barbecue units and started plumping down the prepared burgers, creating hissing sounds and whispers of smoke and the enticing aroma of dinner—at least the potential of dinner.

She didn't know why she suddenly looked up. Tucker was in the middle of laughing, saying something to Pete. Only out of the blue, he stopped talking…and his eyes met hers.

He seemed to freeze up, go still. So did she.

The night they'd made love was suddenly there…as if the space between them suddenly glowed with those memories. The wonder of touch. *His* touch. The textures of him, the smell of him, the tastes of him.

There was something about him. She couldn't hold back from Tucker. Couldn't hold back anything. She'd been as vulnerable as she'd ever been in her life—he'd taken that vulnerability, he'd demanded it—but he'd also protected it by giving back everything he had, everything he was. He'd been as vulnerable as she'd been.

And she wanted him again.

From the dark sheen in his gaze, she knew he wanted her, too. Now. Immediately. Forget everyone else, everything else, forget sense and priorities and work and life and everything else.

When he looked at her that way… But that was just the point. No one ever looked at her the way Tucker did.

No one ever made her feel the way Tucker made her feel.

Sudden shrieks of *"Mom!"* and *"Dad!"* yanked her gaze away from Tucker.

Smoke billowed from her barbecue…and his. She'd never noticed the smell, noticed the smoke, until their sons yelled at the top of their lungs.

The adults at the judging picnic table were cracking up—not with alarm, but laughter.

The first batch of burgers—from both teams—went straight to the trash.

The boys insisted on cooking the next batch, and because neither Tucker nor Garnet thought it was a good idea for their sons to handle the fires alone, the adults took no end of teasing, razzing and grief.

Eventually enough burgers had been cooked—perfectly, as the boys repeated endlessly—after which, Tucker and Garnet got a new round of joshing from the adults at the picnic table.

At one point, she looked at Tucker for the first time since that bonfire moment, and said, "Boy, this is really fun. I'm so glad you invited your family."

Which made them crack up more. Ike was laughing so hard, he had to hold his stomach. "She fits right in," he gasped to Tucker.

"I'm still trying to figure out why we're getting all this grief, when y'all are getting a free dinner. Not to mention the best burgers on the planet."

"They are," Walker agreed, and with a glance at the two boys added, "Did you two sample each other's burgers?"

Both boys nodded.

"So which do you think is the best?"

"The ones I made with Mrs. G.," Will said promptly.

"The ones I made with Mr. T.," Pete said at the same time.

"Uh-oh," Rosemary murmured under breath.

"I'm glad it's on the rest of you instead of us who has to judge this," Tucker said. "So which team wins?"

"Go wander away," Ike told the boys. "We'll vote and then call when we've got the results."

"Can we can go as far as the creek?" Will asked his dad.

"Sure. No sweat. Don't be gone forever, though. A half hour at most." Tucker glanced at Garnet to see if she was okay with that timing. She nodded.

She'd been so wary of coming to this barbecue, so sure Tucker's family would judge her the way her own family did. Tucker had never suggested they were snobs. She just expected that they'd fret over who she was, what she did, her lack of education—all that kind of rigamarole—if they thought she was involved with Tucker. Family protected each other. It was just human nature.

Instead, they were easy to be with. Really easy. Until they were nearly finished with dinner, and the votes on the winning burger team were being discussed.

"I think it's cut and dried. Will and Garnet's burgers were by far the best, with some kind of interesting flavors I'd never..." It was Walker speaking, when his cell phone set off a drum roll.

His wife's cell jangled at the same time.

Both senior MacKinnons immediately rose from the table, with regretful apologies, and quick hugs. But that fast, they were gone, their car zooming out of sight before Garnet could draw a breath or ask a question.

For a few minutes, the group continued as if the senior MacKinnons' leaving didn't matter. The voting discussion on the burger competition finally reached a conclusion. Will and Garnet were announced the winners, with the prize being the same that Petie and Tucker had won in the kayak competition.

And that was all hunky-dory, Garnet thought—except that the whole mood of the gathering had suddenly and drastically changed. No one was laughing and ribbing and talking over each other. Silence infested the group. Tucker's face looked wooden. Smiles looked glued in place. All the energy and enthusiasm in the group had popped like a punctured balloon.

As if emphasizing the bewildering change of mood, a clap of thunder suddenly echoed in the west. The wild wind was pushing in fat clouds. Leaves hurled in the air, bringing the first spatter of raindrops.

Everybody jumped to their feet. Tucker hustled toward the truck, headed for the creek to pick up the kids. Ike aimed for the barbecues to shut them down, and Garnet joined Rosemary to scoop up food and picnic debris as fast as they could. They'd made the first trip into the house before another crack of thunder shook the trees, and the spatter of fat raindrops turned into a hissing, soaking deluge.

By the time Tucker's truck pulled in, they were all soaked, and the sky had turned blacker than midnight. Garnet searched Tucker's face when he stomped in the door—but his expression looked as wooden as it had before. He pushed off shoes, made the boys push off theirs. The only people talking were the boys, who chattered nonstop about the cool thunder and the minnows in the creek and what a great day it was.

"Mom," Pete asked her, "we need to stay a little longer, okay? Because Will and I wanna talk about how to spend his money."

"You really think he needs help with that?" Garnet asked wryly.

"He does. In lots of things, he's better at stuff than me. But not about money. He's not a finance kind of guy."

Garnet suppressed a chuckle at Pete's earnest tone, but she excused the kids to head for the den and the TV. The adults clustered in the kitchen, putting things away, making trash disappear. Garnet tried to make conversation, but she could barely take her eyes off Tucker.

He hustled around them all, filling in, doing his share—he squeezed Rosemary's shoulder, exchanged a quiet glance with Ike. Garnet already guessed there was some serious family thing going on, but she wasn't worried about his brother and sister. Tucker looked... locked up, as if he'd turned a key on some emotional door and bolted it.

Outside, the storm screamed and blew, rain battering the windows like orchestral drums, the lights flickering more than once.

"I've got a generator," Tucker told them all. "And you all know there are enough bedrooms in the place to sleep an army. But it looks as if it's going to blow over. Clearing in the west."

Rosemary stood in the west window, hands on hips. "Clearing? Where? You're dreaming."

"I'm your older brother, remember? I know everything. You're just the brat."

Rosemary slugged him. Ike said, "I do think it's letting up."

"That's because you men always side together! Garnet! Get over here. Tell me if *you* see an ounce of clearing in the west."

"I don't have to look. I'm on Rosemary's side. Whatever she says is right," Garnet called from the kitchen.

"That's it. You have to marry my brother. Take Ike if you won't marry Tucker. It's the only way I'm ever going to get a balance in this family. We need more *female* votes."

Tucker's eyes shot to hers. Hers shot to his right back. It was the *marry* word that created a bolt of lightning between them. Right in the living room. As if the storm had abruptly moved inside. As if the household had disappeared except for the two of them.

Thankfully, they were the only ones that seemed to notice. Ike was praising Rosemary for not "biting" when their parents brought up her broken engagement. Rosemary praised him right back for their parents suggesting Ike could be a better surgeon than either of them were, instead of doing the "kind of doctoring" he'd chosen.

Tucker disappeared for a few minutes to check out the generator in the lean-to behind the cabin. The downpour was starting to lighten up, but that didn't mean clear sailing for certain. They could still lose power. Trees could be down anywhere because of the wind. Mountain storms often blew up hot and fast in the summer.

Within an hour, though, Ike and Rosemary were aiming for the door, determined to drive home. Rosemary popped back in to give both Garnet and her big brother an extra hug.

As the door closed, Garnet suddenly felt edgy and odd. It was just…they'd said goodbye to the guests as if they were an old married couple, and now they were distinctly alone. Before Tucker could say a word, she announced, "I'm going to track down my Pete, and we'll be out of your hair lickety-split, too."

Chapter Twelve

Her plan was to escape faster than the speed of light. She had her bag and van keys in hand when she went searching for Pete. She found him.

And that fast, her escape plan took a nosedive.

She hadn't seen the den in Tucker's house before. The room was dark, with a giant TV dominating one wall. A pair of old couches nested at angles, with a thick rug in between.

Both boys had undoubtedly planned to stay up all night, but Will was sprawled on the rug with a pillow, buried under a light blanket. And her Petie was sleeping just as hard, burrowed into the couch with only a foot peeking out from under a blanket.

"Don't wake him." Tucker's voice came from just behind her, an intimate whisper. "They can sleep right here. Why wake Pete for nothing?"

"But—"

"I can either bring him over in the morning. Or you can stay here, too."

She turned around so swiftly she almost hit her head on the doorjamb. He raised an eyebrow. "Hey. There are a half-dozen spare rooms here. I wasn't suggesting monkey business. I was saying…there could be trees down after a wild storm like that, problems with cars stalled on the road. Why not wait to drive home until daylight?"

She looked again at Pete, who was sleeping so soundly. She rubbed her arms, looking back at Tucker again, still indecisive.

"Now, I know you trust me," he said, in a voice no woman would trust. "So I'll tell you what. My room's at the far right on the second floor." He motioned to the wide staircase. "Will normally sleeps at the room at the top of the stairs." Again he motioned. "There are three spare bedrooms over to the left. Two of them have attached bathrooms." Another motion. "You can pick any one of them. Back when this was a lodge for family gatherings, we set up the rules—fresh linens and blankets in the closet, no point in making up a bed until we know someone's staying. In the meantime, we'll leave the downstairs lights on for the kids. I'll head up first, so you'll know I'm all tucked in and you're safe as church."

"You're sounding a little patronizing," she said irritably.

"That's because I think it should be a real easy decision to make on a night like this."

"Now you're being honestly annoying."

He threw up his hands, in the classic male what-can-you-do-with-women gesture. Really, Garnet thought, it was amazing women hadn't killed men off a long, long time ago…or maybe it was just Tucker who could be this insufferable.

He went upstairs first, just like he'd said. She turned off their TV, turned off a few lights, put a couple of glasses in his dishwasher. By the time she stood at the bottom of the wide staircase again, there was a light under a closed door upstairs. His bedroom.

She took two steps up, then hesitated. She didn't have deodorant or toothpaste, nothing to prepare for an overnight stay. But darn it, Tucker was right. She was exhausted. Petie was settled. It would be downright dumb to take off this late. She'd undoubtedly crash the instant her head found a pillow.

She tiptoed up, crossed the hall to the farthest room, groped for a light and then…inhaled. It was a corner room with big old windows, a four-poster bed with an old-fashioned quilt and feather pillows. Adorable. An armoire held bedding—old, soft sheets, spare towels and blankets.

The adjacent bathroom was done in white tile with red towels; a white terry-cloth robe hung from a hook. Basic toiletries filled a wicker bowl—nothing fancy, just a toothbrush, small tubes of toothpaste and shampoo, miniature deodorant. The shower and sink had white ceramic handles, and the hardwood floor was covered with a big, plush red rug.

Everything was tidy—like Tucker. Very unlike her. Still, it only took her five minutes to destroy the place—throwing off clothes, making up the bed, steaming up the bathroom in a nice, hot shower. While she was drying off—wearing the white terry-cloth robe—she had the bad, bad feeling that the evening wasn't over yet.

She still had time to show very poor judgment. To make an impulsive decision that had frightening and difficult consequences. To act before she'd thoroughly considered the repercussions.

She was so good at doing those things that she readily recognized the signs. The way her heart was pounding. The way her jaw looked stubbornly set in the mirror. The way her nerves were even more jittery than before.

The way she opened the bedroom door, tightening the robe's sash, as she walked barefoot across the long, wide hall.

The way she knocked.

Because a woman looking for trouble always found it, Tucker answered in less than a millisecond. Apparently he'd had the same idea she'd had—about cleaning up—because his hair was still wet from a shower.

Where she was completely concealed in the giant robe, though, Tucker just had a black towel hooked low around his waist. His bare chest was still damp.

He'd half shaved.

He cocked his head when he saw her, as if surprised, but that was foolishness. She was the only one likely to be knocking on his door. He knew it was her…and the expression in his eyes mapped out that a bad, bad mistake was on his mind, too.

"Glad you decided to stay," he said, in a voice rustier than wind.

"I'm really tired. But I knew I wouldn't sleep until I got a couple questions off my chest."

"Right. Come on in."

"I can ask them from right here."

"Whatever works for you," he said, as casual as if they'd had conversations in his bedroom a million times. He grabbed a short towel to dry his hair while she tried to get her vocal cords working.

His bedroom was bigger than the spare, had two sets

of French doors leading to the second-story veranda. His four-poster was king-size. He didn't seem to go for much furniture, which meant the massive bed just naturally seemed to draw the eye.

At least her eyes.

She heard Tucker taking a step, and whipped around again. His hair was now dry—or dry enough—so he'd tossed the towel in the bathroom sink, and met her eyes with a grin on his face.

"I was thinking," she said, and then stopped because that was such a total lie. She wasn't. She wasn't thinking. She knew it. He probably knew it, too. "Don't you think it's interesting? How well our sons get along? When they're so completely different?"

"You bet. They look like Mutt and Jeff when they're walking along together. I haven't figured it out." He cocked his head. "Hey, I didn't congratulate you on winning the burger contest."

"It was Will who did all the work."

"I doubt that."

"Tucker…I was glad you warned me. About what happens when he visits his mother. I almost had to pry a smile out of him with needle-nose pliers. It's not as if he were cranky or rude exactly. He just didn't seem… connected. Engaged."

"I never thought of it in those words, but you nailed it. He always comes back disconnected. Like a turtle without its shell. He wanders around as if he's looking for his life again."

"But he got over it. Really had fun, making the burgers."

"Uh-huh," Tucker said, and then stood there. Silent. Waiting to hear what she really came for.

She felt like a fool, still standing in the doorway like

a prissy goose. So she walked in, sort of wandered, trying to look—and feel—at ease. As far as she could tell, this was the only room in the house he'd completely carpeted. It was dark red, plush beneath her bare feet. "I wanted to ask you about your family. About what happened at dinner."

"What do you mean?"

Was he being facetious? It didn't seem like him. "Tucker. Your parents both got paged by the hospital. They had to leave. Until then, as far as I could tell, your whole family was having a blast together—laughing and teasing and just plain having fun. Then your mom and dad left…and our boys were still okay…but you three siblings shut down as if you'd been thrown in a freezer."

He frowned. "I don't remember that happening."

"Okay. I didn't mean to intrude on something that was none of my business. It just really troubled me at the time. The three of you didn't say anything, but you all seemed upset."

"That's kind of funny." He adjusted the towel, which was sinking to a fascinating level. At least until he re-knotted it. He hooked a hip on the edge of a sleek walnut dresser. "I thought the parents were on their best behavior. Didn't hound Rosemary about her broken engagement. Didn't bore us all today with old stories about family traditions at the lodge. They obviously liked you from the start. And Pete. Not that I'm surprised."

"Tucker, I'm asking about you. Not me."

He glanced out the French doors, as if something amazing had shown up in the darkness in the last two minutes, ambled over there. His butt was tighter than hers. It was another thing that annoyed her about him.

But his was so cute.

The rest of him was so alpha guy. The whole outdoor, brawny thing he had going on all the time. The way he walked and moved and talked, all had that invisible frame of testosterone. But his butt. He had such a little flat butt.

Her eyes shot back to his face when he turned around. "I can't think of a Christmas or a Thanksgiving or a birthday where our parents actually stayed through a whole day. They're terrific surgeons. Even when we were squirt-size, we got it. They were important people. They had the power to save lives. Their work came first."

"And you kids felt as if you always came second," she said gently.

"We *did* come in second. They love us. We love them. But all our lives…if one of us had a scrape, we just bandaged each other up. If Rosemary had a nightmare, she'd come wake me. If Ike got in trouble at school, I'd write the note to excuse him. When Ike broke his arm in football, I took him to the hospital, stayed with him, no different than Rosemary'd open up the Campbell's soup when I had the mother of all flus. Of course she served it cold."

He said it like a joke…and she smiled. But it wasn't funny, the image he'd created in her head, and her heart. Of a lonely Tucker. Of the oldest sibling feeling responsible for the other two.

"You couldn't depend on your parents."

"It didn't matter. We knew we could depend on each other. It worked out fine for all of us. It was just today… It was a get-together for the kids. Your son, my son. They think the sun rises and sets on Will, couldn't wait to be part of this, and then—"

"It was a déjà vu thing. History repeating itself."

"It didn't matter. I didn't notice either of the boys troubled by it in any way."

She doubted the grandparents' swift departure bothered Will or Pete, either. But it mattered to Tucker.

Her throat suddenly felt thick. Her heart picked up some kind of weird-sick rhythm, as if she was looking at a mountain of hurt. Maybe she was. She readily understood why Tucker might be wild enough to climb mountains and do daredevil kayaking and get a charge from that kind of excitement. But deep down, in his heart, he wanted safe. Family he could count on. A lover who wasn't unpredictable and impulsive and had a history of making extremely big mistakes.

Like her.

Yeah. Well, right then, she did what she always did. The wrong thing.

He was hurt. He'd shouldered the parenting role for both his siblings. Didn't believe someone else could be there for him. And maybe she was the wrong person to be there forever, but she could be there right now.

She closed the door. Took seven steps across the room, her bare feet sinking into that thick red carpet. Her eyes stayed on his, taking in his suddenly confused expression, the way he tilted his head, opened his mouth—as if he were about to say something...but she got there first.

Or her mouth got there first. Her lips sealed his. Her hands climbed up his bare arms. He smelled of mountain and moonlight and damp clean skin. The feel of him, the texture of him, was everything she'd ever yearned for. He was all the things a woman wasn't. All the things that made her strong.

All the things that made her weak.

He picked up the kiss as if he'd started the madness

and mayhem. No grass ever grew under Tucker's feet. He was always ready, had his pulse on inventive possibilities before she'd even forged a next step. He knew all the steps. Crossed the room in two shakes, leveled her onto the middle of his feather bed, sent pillows skidding to the floor.

"Oh, yeah," he murmured, in that whiskery tone that always stoked her fires. Approval, so hard to win anywhere else in life, was so easy to earn with Tucker. All she had to do was yield. Power and pleasure.

Outside, there was a peek of moon through glistening windows. Where the relentless wind had been intrusive before, now there was a soft silence, light where there'd been darkness. She could hear Tucker's breath, so clearly, getting gruffer. Her fingers combed through his thick dark hair, while she felt the scrape of his half-shaved jaw roughing up the skin at her throat, then down to the valley between her breasts.

If his breath conveyed urgency and impatience, the wash of his tongue was luxuriously slow, easy, a wraparound tingle that she felt clear to her toes.

She'd had a robe on. Belted on. Yet somehow he'd made it go away, so there was nothing between his skin and hers. Where breast touched breast, tummy touched tummy, fingers touched anywhere and everywhere... and sparks of flame seemed to light up the night. She couldn't lay still, not with that kind of burn.

She had to move, to kiss him back, stroke him back, press tighter, promise more. Demand more.

"You ready to climb mountains?" he murmured.

"With you." The answer was so easy.

"No anchors. No safety nets. No fail-safes."

"With you," she whispered again, because that was

how it would always be with Tucker. No giving half-way. No maybes or conditions.

He slid inside her, smooth and easy, the fit closer than a surgeon's glove. He filled her up, beyond what she could take, yet her greedy gasp of pleasure said otherwise. She wanted all of Tucker. Every inch, every molecule.

He tucked her legs up tight around his waist, started the climb, slow and tantalizing at first, then moving into music, a rhythm echoed in heartbeats.

On that fast, sweaty, glorious race to the top, she heard a splintered groan from him. He was waiting, waiting for her to reach the top before he did. She loved that agonized sound. It propelled her into a toboggan slide uphill, up a mountain, up somewhere near Tucker's heart...and hers.

It was still the black velvet time of night, but she didn't know how much time had passed. One of them showed no inclination to sleep. There'd been a lazy pattern of smooches. Nuzzles. Tickles.

"Are you going to let a girl sleep, Tucker?"

"Are you kidding? No."

"You're a bad, bad man."

"Thank you."

Well, that required her to rouse. At least a little. "Thank you," she whispered back.

"Hey. Garnet?"

"Yes, it's me. I'm pretty sure there are no other women in your bed."

Her fingertip traced his smile, but then he nipped it. "I love you. I can't remember if I told you before. I've known it for quite a while. And I've said it in my head a thousand times. But I'm not dead sure if I happened to tell you."

"You didn't."

"Well, don't panic. It's only love." And that time he kissed her, so deep and dark and sweetly, that she couldn't talk for a long time after that.

Tucker woke the same time he always did, when the dawn was just peeking over the horizon, mist swirling around the trees, birds just starting to stir. He faced the east, always slept that way, but immediately turned toward Garnet.

His sleepy smile died. She wasn't there. She'd edged two pillows against his back, keeping him warm, making him think she was still sleeping next to him. But the sheet beside him was cool.

He'd never heard a car, never heard a footstep or a door opening and closing...but then, likely he wouldn't have. She'd worn him out after the second round of lovemaking. Maybe he was usually a light sleeper, but he'd crashed completely last night, still wrapped around her.

He pushed off the comforter, climbed out of bed. It didn't have to mean anything "bad" that she was gone. She had a business to run. Probably needed to get there early, before the staff showed up, and she might have wakened Pete, just to make sure her son didn't wake up and go wandering to find his mom.

Or, she could be downstairs right now. Making coffee. Waiting for the household to get up to share breakfast.

But somehow he knew that wasn't the deal.

She was gone.

He did a fast wash-up, pulled on clothes and charged downstairs, first toward the den, then toward the kitchen. In the den, he didn't need to switch on a light to see that Pete was gone, and his Will was still sprawled on the couch, sleeping hard, blankets all a tangle.

The kitchen was another story. He switched on the overhead, and realized immediately there'd been an intruder in the night. There were no dirty dishes in the sink, not even glasses. The vandal had cleaned the counter, did something to make the sink shine within an inch of its life, even swept the damn floor.

He opened the back door, and with hands on hips just stood there, taking in the milky morning, the pale light just stroking the edge of the trees, the deck with dew…and her van distinctly gone.

She had a business to run, he reminded himself again. She had every reason to leave early. It didn't have to mean anything troublesome.

But he *was* troubled.

He should never have told her he loved her. She didn't believe people loved her. She didn't see herself as lovable. She saw herself differently than the entire rest of the world saw her.

When he'd mentioned that four-letter word, it hadn't been impulsive, hadn't been because of the heat and wonder of lovemaking. He'd thought she was ready to hear it. He'd thought, sooner or later, they had to get past that boulder, or how could they progress beyond being lovers? And as lovers—with two sons far too observant to fool for long—they couldn't make it. It had to be all or nothing.

For him, maybe it always had to be all or nothing. He wanted a wife. A love-mate. Someone to wake up to, to argue with, to laugh and work with. To make love to, easily and often, rough and soft, fast and endlessly slow and all the variations possible in a loving relationship.

He'd feared she'd panic. She was just so wary of the *L* word.

So he had a choice. To honor her silence, her choice of distance.

Or to confront her head-on, no holds barred, risk the whole world and winner take all.

It wasn't really a choice or a decision. Tucker knew the minute he woke up exactly what he intended to do.

Chapter Thirteen

A carload of women pulled into the yard, just as a fresh pot of coffee finished brewing.

Garnet needed the whole pot before diving into a crazy Monday.

Pete had fallen back asleep the minute they got home, but Garnet knew how much had to be done today. Maybe her mind and heart were on Tucker, but she couldn't just run around being in love with the damn man. Bills *had* to be paid today. Vanilla needed to be harvested. Money had to go to the bank. The cooking herbs needed misting, and other herbs needed drying—and in this heat, when things were ready...they were *ready*.

She unlocked the shop door and let the carload of ladies inside. Steam was already coming off the pavement, a mix of the wet from yesterday's rain and plain old summer heat. It was definitely going to be a scorcher.

She charged around unlocking and straightening, setting up the cash register, opening the shades. Mary Lou showed up five minutes early wearing dark capris and a fawn top, scowling at the customers. "Where's the fire?" she barked, because she never liked to open early and didn't think Garnet ever should.

"No fire," she said brightly.

"Something's wrong." Mary Lou stalked over to peer into her face. "You all right?"

"Mostly. I didn't get a lot of sleep last night, so I might need to mainline some coffee."

"That's not what's wrong." Mary Lou poured her first mug of coffee and carted it with her as she began her start-up chores, but while Garnet handled the church ladies, she found Mary Lou staring at her again.

"You aren't *happy,* are you?"

"Pardon?"

"I was still trying to figure what's odd about you this morning. Is that it? That you're *happy?*"

"It couldn't be," Garnet assured her, and cut the ridiculous conversation short. Two cars and an SUV pulled into the drive. What was this? The craziest Monday of the whole year?

Tucker called when she had a frazzling fourteen customers in the store—Mary Lou was still hiding in the back, and Sally hadn't shown up yet. He called the shop landline, so she didn't know it was him until she heard that low, wicked voice.

"You told my kid he could have two kittens? Without asking me?"

"Yes, Mr. MacKinnon, I did. So don't blame Will."

"I wasn't blaming him. I just couldn't believe you did that."

"I can't, either. I knew it was dead wrong."

"Did I ever mention that I've never been a cat person?"

"Well, darn it, Tucker, I wasn't, either. She showed up pregnant. It was too late to give her the facts-of-life lecture."

"Like that's an excuse. There is going to be payback," he threatened, and hung up.

She started breathing again. Had there been yearning in his voice? Or hers? Was his call really about a love song, or was he really thinking about cats? When he'd muttered about payback right before hanging up, had he said it in a loving, crooning voice? Her pulse seemed to think he had.

"Hey, Mom." Petie ducked around customers, ambling in her direction.

"What's up?"

"Nothing, really. I just stopped to tell you I was going to make something cool for lunch. Like peanut butter and bacon. And maybe brownies."

"That sounds terrific."

"Oh. One more thing. I figured you might want to know. The washing machine started shaking all over."

"What?"

Petie turned back around. "It's no biggie. I shut it off. I just thought I should tell you. It was shaking and shooting suds all over the place. It was really funny for a couple of minutes."

Garnet called for Mary Lou to take over, grabbed a phone book to get her repair man's number and hit the back door aiming for home. The washing machine was old. She'd gotten it used to start with, but it had been an angel…mostly. Every machine got crabby once in a while, didn't it?

She sprinted into the laundry room, gasped, then

reached for her cell phone. It wasn't in her shorts pocket. Wasn't on the counter. She couldn't find her purse, but she was pretty sure she hadn't left it there. "Pete!" she called, and started searching for him.

As she should have expected, he was holed up in front of the computer with a banana peel and a giant glass of milk next to him. He didn't respond to her voice, just raised the cell phone so she could see it.

"In the next life, I'm going to remember everything and you're going to be the one to lose stuff."

"Uh-huh."

She'd just dialed the number when she noticed a battered Grand Am parked at the house. Sally's car. Sally, who wouldn't be parking at the house on a workday for any reason Garnet could imagine. But then she saw Sally's face in the doorway. Dropped the phone. Forgot the phone. Just rushed to bring Sally inside.

Sally wasn't crying. Garnet had never seen her cry. But this time the right side of Sally's face was swollen to the point of breaking skin, her right eye invisible, her lip cracked, and she was walking as if every step caused her pain.

"I'll be taking you to the hospital," Garnet said swiftly and sharply.

"No."

"And I'm calling the police."

"No."

"Sally, I'm not talking to you as an employer. I'm talking to you as a friend. I'm not listening to 'no.' Not again. Never again."

"That's why I came here." Sally rested an arm on the counter, as if she needed the support. "My kids are at my sister's. They're safe. But you told me about this shelter before. But you know my car. He knows my car. So I was hoping you might drive me. Garnet, I know it's a workday. That the shop's open. That Mary Lou could tick off any and every customer if she has a chance. But I thought…maybe I could just stay here until after the shop closes. I could drive the car behind the greenhouses, way out of sight. I don't want to put you or Petie in danger. I just—"

"Quit. We'll go right now. Although I still think you should see a doctor first."

"Nothing's broken." Sally leaned hard against the counter. "Believe me, I'd know."

Garnet grabbed her van keys, told Petie where she was going, ran back to the shop to tell a mightily annoyed Mary Lou that she had to be gone and helped Sally into the van. She knew where to take her, because two years ago she'd talked to a policewoman when she'd been trying to track down help for Sally that time. Sally had just never been willing to take advantage before.

The place was halfway to Greenville, dodging traffic all the way. "Do you want to tell me what happened?"

Sally had her head leaned back, eyes closed. She'd tried to put on the seat belt, but couldn't. "No point. Nothing to tell I hadn't told before."

"Okay. But I need to tell you…I'm proud of you."

"Look at me. Haven't done one thing in my life that I can be proud of."

"Yeah, you have. You're rescuing one of the best women I know."

"Oh, shut up, Garnet. You're always telling me crap like that."

"You can count on it," Garnet promised her.

The address she had wasn't for the specific shelter, but only a transfer point, because the true shelter location was kept secret. Obviously that only made sense, but it was still hard for Garnet to just drop her friend there, carry in the small satchel Sally had taken with her and give her a careful hug.

"I hate deserting you in the middle of the busy season," Sally said.

"And I'll miss you. But you're totally doing the right thing, and you know it."

Driving back to Plain Vanilla, though, Garnet had to gulp. Handling the shop with just Mary Lou for help was going to be beyond challenging. Obviously she could hire someone new, but even if the perfect person showed up, it would take time and training to get them up to speed.

She zoomed back into the yard by 1:00 p.m., saw the crowd of customers, saw Mary Lou with her hands on her hips arguing with one of them…and waded into the swarm. Mary Lou barked that she was taking lunch, and galloped toward the back of the shop where she could work without having to talk to anyone—her favorite thing. And Garnet's favorite thing, besides working with the herbs, was being with the customers, but she couldn't catch a free minute until almost three.

Then she remembered the crisis with the washing machine. Dialed the repair number while she was hiking toward the house to find out how Pete was faring. The number rang three times before a man's voice answered, soft and low.

"Hey. I almost didn't answer, but then I saw your number on the screen. Glad you called."

"Tucker?"

His voice lost some of that soft, low sexy stuff. "Who'd you think you were calling?"

"Arthur. Darn it. I'm sorry, I—"

"Wait a minute. *Who* is Arthur?"

"Not like that, Tucker. And I'm sorry times a million. I'll call you as soon as I can. Still today. Promise. But I *have* to go." She hung up. Mentally kicked herself. Then looked up the real number for Arthur and reached him, and although he didn't think he could come until Thursday, at least he was scheduled—so she could turn her mind back to more immediate crises.

Sally had a whiteboard in Plain Vanilla's back room, with her schedule of jobs...like the thirty-five lavender and rose-hip sachets that were ordered for tomorrow.

Tomorrow.

Then there was the recipe book—Garnet's idea, but Sally was almost finished putting it together. The goal was to have it on sale in the shop by next week. They'd advertised.

Garnet figured she'd manage to get that done the same day cows flew.

"Look." Mary Lou pounced the minute she showed up in back. "You know I'll do anything you ask. But people don't like me. And I don't like them. And I can have the front four acres mowed in less than an hour, so why don't you just stay here and I'll pretend to be actually useful for the rest of the day."

"Okay." What else could she say?

By the time she closed the shop at six, she was lightheaded and exhausted. She still had to handle bills, check on the vanilla, see if she could find some help to take Sally's place. Pete was prowling around the kitchen.

"Hey," he said. "I've still got your bacon and peanut butter sandwich. You didn't show up for lunch."

"Couldn't," she admitted. "What do you feel like for dinner?"

"Burgers and fries."

"How about Cordon Bleu and some noodles?" She added, "But I need to call Tucker before I get started—"

"I already talked to Mr. Tucker."

"You did. Why?"

"Because I left my hat at his house. You know. My Duke University hat. He said he found it. Then I told him about the washing machine turning into a volcano. He laughed. Then said he had a big group just showing up, so I talked to Will. He wants to spend his money at Best Buy. His dad said it was okay about him getting two kittens, he said. But I think I should be able to keep two then, too."

"No."

"Well, at least *one*."

"No."

"We'll talk about it later," Pete assured her, using the time-honored adult voice that meant he wasn't about to give in.

She still wanted to talk to Tucker…badly, badly wanted to talk with Tucker. But there was dinner and then a help-wanted ad to create, and then there were the bills. Two were overdue. Not because she couldn't pay them, but because she just kept forgetting. Pete hung out for a few minutes, wanting to tell her what the kittens had been up to today, wanting to explain a game that was completely over her head, but she loved listening to him and couldn't possibly cut her son short when he wanted to talk.

Finally, Petie wore down. She brewed a fresh pot of coffee and parked in front of the stack of bills and her computer and ledgers. She liked bookkeeping on a par with poison ivy, but she tucked a leg under her and settled down. The sun dropped. She turned on a lamp.

The mother cat wandered in, brushed against her leg, settled down with a noisy purr.

When the phone rang, she jumped, then grabbed it. "Tucker," she began…but it wasn't Tucker.

"It's me, honey."

"Dad! How terrific for you to call. How's everything going?" She twisted back, cocked a bare leg on the desk, smiling. Her mom stopped in and called all the time, but she rarely had dad-time anymore.

"Your mom got on me. Said you and I were overdue a chat."

"We are! I'm so glad you called!" But her exuberance slowly faded as her dad continued on.

"Your mother said there was a new man in your life. Said he came from a good family of doctors. Lots of heritage in that MacKinnon family name."

"Yes. I guess thcrc is," she said slowly. She squeezed her eyes closed, not wanting to hear more.

"Relieved to hear you've got a good man on the hook, honey. You've had a hard time finding your way. Your sisters both had it easier. I always felt your struggles were my fault."

"Nothing was your fault."

"I failed to protect you."

"I didn't need—"

"Now, honey, I know you're from a different generation. But some things really haven't changed since the beginning of time, not for men and women. You fell so hard for Johnny. Way too young. I should have been paying attention."

"Dad, trust me. No one and nothing could have stopped me from doing anything."

"Well, I think I could have. I think I should have. Teenagers just aren't old enough to realize that even one mistake can be serious, alter the path of your life forever."

Her throat clogged. Damned if she was going to cry. "I know I didn't take the life path you wanted me to, but honestly, I'm fine."

"Of course you're fine. You're beautiful and strong and a wonderful mother. But if this man is the financial prospect that your mother says—well, I'm just saying, be careful, honey. Don't blow it. Your sisters so easily found their place in the sun. Now you've finally got your shot."

When Garnet hung up, initially she felt the same response she always felt after dealing with her family. She'd failed them. They all believed she didn't come close to measuring up to the woman she could have been. They never said they were ashamed of her, but it was there in every conversation, soft and sneaky and framed in kind, loving words.

That knee-jerk response faded this time. Garnet wasn't positive as to why she didn't buy in this time, but she feared it was something to do with Tucker. And even though she was more tired than a whipped puppy, she knew she'd never sleep until she'd thought this through.

Tucker jammed the keys in the truck, slammed on the lights, slapped the gearshift into Drive and aimed down the mountain.

Hey. Garnet had every right to have dozens of male friends. There was no reason in the universe she couldn't have a special friend named Arthur.

It's not as if Tucker had put a ring on her finger. No, they hadn't discussed commitment—but he re-ally thought she got it. That they were two halves of a whole. That they had an irreplaceable connection with each other.

That—just like the corny fairy tales—the earth actually moved when they touched. When they just looked at each other. And for damn sure, when they made love.

Two spots of light showed on the side of the road. A buck. Tucker wanted to get to her fast, but he immediately slowed down. He'd never been an emotional driver before. He'd never had an angry temperament. And he wasn't mad now.

He was just a little...testy.

Once he got there, he'd find her, initiate a tactful, genial discussion. Maybe start with a joke. Just casually mention the name Arthur. Convey that he was cool about her knowing this Arthur guy. A total no-sweat.

His cell buzzed. His newer truck had the super no-hands feature for cell calls. Will's voice came on, full of cheer. "Everything's totally fine, Dad. I talked to Pete. He's fine, too. I'm fine. He's fine. Everybody's fine."

"Huh? You're sounding mighty weird."

"Oh, no. I just wanted to tell you not to worry. Pete's already in bed at his house. I'm going to bed right now." A fake yawn bellowed through the cell line. "Man, I'm really beat. Pete said he was, too."

"What are you *talking* about?"

"Nothing. I was just calling to tell you that I'm fine, that I'm going to sleep this very second. That I'll call Uncle Ike if I need anything. But I won't. So if you're gone a while, it's a big no-sweat. It's a big no-sweat for Pete, too."

"Is there a bad connection here? Where's my son? Because whomever I'm talking to isn't making a lick of sense. I'll be home inside of an hour, like I told you."

"Right, Dad." His son clicked off. Tucker shook his

head in bafflement, but not for long. Will might be having a demented moment, but in every way that mattered, he was fine. Tucker needed to concentrate on the crisis at hand.

No one else was driving the mountain road but him. The truck lights kept finding critter eyes. Raccoon. Deer. Damned if there wasn't a cougar in the brush at the ridge. The variety of wildlife would have fascinated him—on another night.

Tonight there was only one thing on his mind.

He pulled into her drive, dropping his lights to dim, realizing abruptly that the shop, the house—everything—was lights-off black. No surprise. It was after eleven. He was the only one so revved up and wide-awake that he'd never even glanced at his watch before taking off.

His heart thudding, he slowly reversed…but then caught a pale glow of light in the distance. Her greenhouses and shade houses were all shut down—except for the far one, her precious vanilla greenhouse. So someone was up…and that someone had to be Garnet.

He parked, sprinted toward the greenhouse in the dark, knocked on the external door. It wasn't locked. And when no one immediately responded, he just opened the door and stepped in.

At first, he just saw the lush rain forest, green on green, the place dominated by loamy, rich scents and the lushness of growth. Garnet's head popped up in the middle of all that jungle…and just like that, his heart settled down.

Until that instant, he didn't know how desperately he needed to see her. How much wasn't right, could never be right again, unless he was with her.

Her hair was a tangled mess, kerchiefed to keep away

from her face. She had a smudge of dirt on her cheek, another on a bare shoulder. She was just wearing a camisole, nothing underneath, maybe because it was warm in here, maybe because she never expected to see anyone anyway. But when she popped to her feet, the startled expression on her face changed immediately when she spotted him.

The look in her eyes was lush with yearning. Sharp with fear. Liquid with love.

"I was just driving by," he said, "and I thought I'd stop in, maybe say hi, ask you about Arthur."

"Arthur?" she asked bewilderedly.

"Yeah. You know. The Arthur you were trying to reach when you called me by mistake this afternoon? I was just wondering…well, what you thought of him. How long you've known him. Is he a good friend. That kind of thing."

"Well…" She dusted her hands on the back of her shorts, then waded her way through the thick, fragrant greenery like Tarzan's Jane ambling through the jungle. She looked *so* like a nymph. His nymph. "I've known Arthur from the time I moved here. Pete was a baby then. I didn't have much. Bought a used stove. It ran twice before shorting out. A neighbor told me to call him."

Tucker just stood there, listening, so she went on.

"Arthur took a look, told me to throw the stove out, and not to buy any more used appliances without his approval first. He came back that same day with a horrible-looking olive-green stove that ran perfectly for a good five years. Never charged me a dime. I've always called him if I had a fix-it type problem. Like the washing machine today." She shook her finger. "It's not what you think."

He was getting that impression, but not totally. It was hard to abandon a worry that had kidnapped his heart most of the day. "What's not what I think?" God, he was starting to talk like her. A bad sign.

"Arthur can be a little—how can I put this delicately?—scary. His hair's stark white, long and wild, and he has all these scars. Some on his face and arms. He doesn't see real well out of his one eye, and you can tell he's got arthritis, but if you give him any sympathy, he'll bark your head off. Once you get past that, though..." She cocked her head, clearly conveying that she was unsure how this conversation had come up. "If you need some kind of repairman, I've got his number in the house. It's in the yellow pages, too, I just—"

"That's okay. I don't think I'll need it quite this minute." He sank onto the top of a metal stool. Good thing she had that metal stool by the sinks, because he'd likely have fallen flat in the dirt otherwise. The relief flooding him seemed to have turned his bones to jelly.

"You really needed to know this at eleven o'clock at night?"

"That's not the only thing. I was wondering..."

"What?"

He motioned. "Maybe you could tell me some more about your vanilla. Like what you've just been doing. I know you keep this place locked up. I only saw it before because of the copperhead. But somehow...there's been no time to ask you about what you're doing."

Something changed in her expression. She emerged completely from the rain forest—or what looked to him like a rain forest. She was wearing disgracefully short shorts and had bare feet. Mighty dirty bare feet. And there was a glint in her eye that was slightly...challenging.

"What I've been doing tonight is about sex, Tucker. Are you sure you're up for the lecture? It's pretty tedious to someone who's not interested."

"You can trust me. I'm 100 percent interested."

"Well…" She sashayed past him, turned the faucet in the sink, reached for soap and water. "Here's the story. It's easy enough to grow a vanilla plant, but really hard to get the plant to produce a vanilla bean. I'm afraid the problem is sex. I don't want to shock you, Tucker, so I won't go any further if you're uncomfortable with some graphic terms."

"That's okay. I'm old enough, honest. You want to see my ID?"

"No, no, I trust you. The issue is pollination. A lot of plants pollinate pretty easily, via wind or bees or birds. But my vanilla plants—the vanilla plants that produce offspring in the form of a vanilla bean—they happen to have a girl part, and a boy part."

"I'll be darned. Who'd have thought it?" Suddenly he wasn't feeling so weak. Garnet wouldn't be talking to him like this, looking at him like this, if she were about to give him his walking papers. She was still standing at the sink, wiping her hands with a towel. She'd washed her face, too, but missed a spot. She hopped up onto the counter, still wiping her hands, but her expression he could only describe as downright perky.

"Now, Tucker, I never liked hearing what goes on in someone else's bedroom. It isn't any of my business. But someone has to help the vanilla along. I don't want to explain too much. But basically, to make a baby vanilla bean, we need to have the pollen come in contact with the stigma."

"Uh-oh. This might be over my head."

"I'm sure you can grasp the concept. It takes me—

the matchmaker—to peel back this teensy flap of tissue in order to get some of that special pollen. Now, in human boys, that's called—"

"I know about boys. You don't have to tell me that part."

"Okay. So I scoop up some of that special pollen stuff and smear it all over the stigma. It's a messy, sweaty business, but I love it."

"I know you do."

"See, there's this long tube that goes into the flower. So once the pollen contacts the stigma, it goes down that tube. Deep inside, well, that's where the baby vanilla bean starts growing."

He'd reached her. It took a long time because he'd walked toward her so slowly. Once she perched up on the counter, she'd started swinging her legs. The closer he got, the faster she swung her legs.

He picked up the scrap of towel, brushed the dirt off her cheek that she'd missed. At that point, she went still altogether, her eyes on his. She'd been gutsy and sassy enough moments ago, but now her lips were trembling. Just a little.

"Garnet?" He leaned into her, accidentally managing to part her legs. He touched his forehead to her forehead. "You mentioned a couple of times that you think of yourself as plain vanilla. Ordinary. Not fancy."

"*Yes*. That's me."

"I get it. That that's how you see yourself. But I see you as the rare orchid. Like no other woman. Special. Requiring special care, extra respect, extra cherishing." He tilted his head, homed in for a kiss. The first, he hoped, of several million kisses that night.

"You're delusional," she said gently, when he finally raised his mouth again. Her lips, he noticed, were wet.

No longer trembling. But the pulse in her throat was beating like a drum.

"I'm not delusional."

"I've made some giant-size mistakes."

He nodded. "So have I. Which is precisely why we need to be married. So we can make mistakes together instead of coping alone."

"Tucker! Did you say the *M* word?!"

"Yeah. I said the *L* word first. But you ran. So I figured maybe we should put it all more specifically. Love. Marriage. Living in the same house. Two boys, maybe more. I'll handle your snakes. You handle—"

"Tucker! I can't think when you do that!"

So he had to do it some more. Level more kisses on her, kisses involving tongues and pressure and coming on sipping-slow. Walking his hands on her, rubbing here, kneading there, bringing her closer to him. Closer again. So close her nipples hardened against his chest, and that beating pulse in her throat started to pick up speed like a jackhammer.

He surfaced again. Only for oxygen. "I have a plan," he said thickly.

"Uh-oh. Every time you say, 'I have a plan,' I know there's trouble coming."

"But this is a *good* plan."

"That's what you always say."

"All right, all right. I'll tell you about my plan a little later." He figured he'd soften her up over time. Over a lot of lovemaking. Over a whole lot of love and living together.

"Uh-oh. I forgot to tell you something, Tucker. Something important."

"Hmm?" He heard her, but it seemed mighty unlikely she was in the mood for any more talking. There were telling signs. The way she was running her hands up his shirt. The way she was shifting back and forth, snugging her pelvis tight against him. The way she leaned into, yearned into, cradled into that last kiss.

"I love you."

"I know," he assured her.

"I mean...really love you. Huge love. Real love. Scary love. The whole shebang."

"Yeah. Petrifying, isn't it? So it's extra good that we're doing this love thing together."

She lifted her head, cheeks flushed, lips red—but she was chuckling.

About time, he thought, to lift her to her feet, shut out the lights and aim inside.

Epilogue

On the first day of school, Garnet and Tucker watched the boys join the throng of kids hiking toward the school entrance. Some things were always the same—the kids all looked as if they had new shoes, new book bags and fresh haircuts.

But some things were distinctly different. Middle school had a completely different look than elementary.

"Do you see those *girls?*" she asked Tucker.

"Do you mean the one with the makeup troweled on? Or the one with the skirt hiked up so far I can practically see her underpants." Tucker clawed a hand through his hair. "I'm not sure I'm going to survive middle school."

"We'll do okay. It can't be that bad." Garnet tucked her arm in his as they walked back to the van. "You know how worried we were at the start of the summer? But now I think…we were both crazy. Our boys are totally fine. My Pete is never going to be an athlete. Your

Will isn't likely to turn into an egghead. But they're both happy. With themselves, with who they are."

She lifted her hand—the way she seemed to do accidentally, several times a day. The necklace was new. She'd never been much for fancy jewelry, but this was a simple, long chain of garnets. The stones loved being caught in the sunlight, blazed with warm, soft color. She adored it.

The necklace had been a gift from the boys and Tucker. They'd wanted to give it to her on Christmas, but none of them could wait that long for her to see it. They'd panned for the stones, tumbled them, taken them to a jeweler to have the necklace made.

Her boys, she thought, were the best.

But her man was even more "best."

With a grin she reached over to kiss him. They had heaps to work out yet, but it was all coming together.

She had a plan.

* * * * *

COMING NEXT MONTH from Harlequin®
Special Edition®
AVAILABLE JULY 24, 2012

#2203 PUPPY LOVE IN THUNDER CANYON
Montana Mavericks: Back in the Saddle
Christyne Butler
An intense, aloof surgeon meets his match in a friendly librarian who believes that emotional connections can heal—and she soon teaches him that love is the best medicine!

#2204 THE DOCTOR AND THE SINGLE MOM
Men of Mercy Medical
Teresa Southwick
Dr. Adam Stone picked the wrong place to rent. Or maybe just the wrong lady to rent from. Jill Beck is beloved—and protected—by the entire town. One wrong move with the sexy single mom could cost him a career in Blackwater Lake, Montana—and the chance to fill up the empty place inside him.

#2205 RILEY'S BABY BOY
Reunion Brides
Karen Rose Smith
Feuding families make a surprise baby and even bigger challenges. Are Brenna McDougall and Riley O'Rourke ready for everything life has in store for them? Including a little surpise romance?

#2206 HIS BEST FRIEND'S WIFE
Gina Wilkins
How much is widowed mom Renae Sanchez willing to risk for a sexy, secretive man from her past...a man she once blamed for her husband's death?

#2207 A WEEK TILL THE WEDDING
Linda Winstead Jones
Jacob Tasker and Daisy Bell think they are doing the right thing when they pretend to still be engaged for the sake of his sick grandmother. But as their fake nuptials start leading to real love, they find out that granny may have a few tricks up her old sleeve!

#2208 ONE IN A BILLION
Home to Harbor Town
Beth Kery
A potential heiress—the secret baby of her mother's affair—is forced by the will to work with her nemesis, a sexy tycoon, to figure out the truth about her paternity, and what it means for the company of which she now owns half!

HSECNM0712

REQUEST YOUR FREE BOOKS!

2 FREE NOVELS PLUS 2 FREE GIFTS!

♦ Harlequin®

SPECIAL EDITION

Life, Love & Family

YES! Please send me 2 FREE Harlequin® Special Edition novels and my 2 FREE gifts (gifts are worth about $10). After receiving them, if I don't wish to receive any more books, I can return the shipping statement marked "cancel." If I don't cancel, I will receive 6 brand-new novels every month and be billed just $4.49 per book in the U.S. or $5.24 per book in Canada. That's a saving of at least 14% off the cover price! It's quite a bargain! Shipping and handling is just 50¢ per book in the U.S. and 75¢ per book in Canada.* I understand that accepting the 2 free books and gifts places me under no obligation to buy anything. I can always return a shipment and cancel at any time. Even if I never buy another book, the two free books and gifts are mine to keep forever.

235/335 HDN FEGF

Name	(PLEASE PRINT)	
Address		Apt. #
City	State/Prov.	Zip/Postal Code

Signature (if under 18, a parent or guardian must sign)

Mail to the **Reader Service:**
IN U.S.A.: P.O. Box 1867, Buffalo, NY 14240-1867
IN CANADA: P.O. Box 609, Fort Erie, Ontario L2A 5X3

Not valid for current subscribers to Harlequin Special Edition books.

Want to try two free books from another line?
Call 1-800-873-8635 or visit www.ReaderService.com.

* Terms and prices subject to change without notice. Prices do not include applicable taxes. Sales tax applicable in N.Y. Canadian residents will be charged applicable taxes. Offer not valid in Quebec. This offer is limited to one order per household. All orders subject to credit approval. Credit or debit balances in a customer's account(s) may be offset by any other outstanding balance owed by or to the customer. Please allow 4 to 6 weeks for delivery. Offer available while quantities last.

Your Privacy—The Reader Service is committed to protecting your privacy. Our Privacy Policy is available online at www.ReaderService.com or upon request from the Reader Service.

We make a portion of our mailing list available to reputable third parties that offer products we believe may interest you. If you prefer that we not exchange your name with third parties, or if you wish to clarify or modify your communication preferences, please visit us at www.ReaderService.com/consumerschoice or write to us at Reader Service Preference Service, P.O. Box 9062, Buffalo, NY 14269. Include your complete name and address.

HSE11B

Harlequin® Super Romance®

*Enjoy a month of compelling, emotional stories, including
a poignant new tale of love lost and found from*

Sarah Mayberry

When Angela Bartlett loses her best friend to a rare heart
condition, it seems only natural that she step in and help
widower and friend Michael Young. The last thing she
expects is to find herself falling for him....

Within Reach

Available August 7!

"I loved it. I thought the story was very believable.
The characters were endearing. The author wrote beautifully...
I will be looking for future books by Sarah Mayberry."

—Sherry, Harlequin® Superromance® reader, on *Her Best Friend*

Find more great stories this month from
Harlequin® Superromance® at

www.Harlequin.com

Angie Bartlett and Michael Robinson are friends. And following the death of his wife, Angie's best friend, their bond has grown even more. But that's all there is…right?

Read on for an exciting excerpt of WITHIN REACH by Sarah Mayberry, available August 2012 from Harlequin® Superromance®.

"HEY. RIGHT ON TIME," Michael said as he opened the door.

The first thing Angie registered was his fresh haircut and that he was clean shaven—a significant change from the last time she'd visited. Then her gaze dropped to his broad chest and the skintight black running pants molded to his muscular legs. The words died on her lips and she blinked, momentarily stunned by her acute awareness of him.

"You've cut your hair," she said stupidly.

"Yeah. Decided it was time to stop doing my caveman impersonation."

He gestured for her to enter. As she brushed past him she caught the scent of his spicy deodorant. He preceded her to the kitchen and her gaze traveled across his shoulders before dropping to his backside. Angie had always made a point of not noticing Michael's body. They were friends and she didn't want to know that kind of stuff. Now, however, she was forcibly reminded that he was a *very* attractive man.

Suddenly she didn't know where to look.

It was then that she noticed the other changes—the clean kitchen, the polished dining table and the living room free of clutter and abandoned clothes.

"Look at you go." Surely these efforts meant he was rejoining life.

He shrugged, but seemed pleased she'd noticed. "Getting there."

They maintained eye contact and the moment expanded. A connection that went beyond the boundaries of their friendship formed between them. Suddenly Angie wanted Michael in ways she'd never felt before. *Ever.*

"Okay. Let's get this show on the road," his six-year-old daughter, Eva, announced as she marched into the room.

Angie shook her head to break the spell and focused on Eva. "Great. Looking forward to a little light shopping?"

"Yes!" Eva gave a squeal of delight, then kissed her father goodbye.

Angie didn't feel 100 percent comfortable until she was sliding into the driver's seat.

Which was dumb. It was nothing. A stupid, odd bit of awareness that meant *nothing.* Michael was still Michael, even if he was gorgeous. Just because she'd tuned in to that fact for a few seconds didn't change anything.

Does Angie's new awareness mark a permanent shift in their relationship? Find out in WITHIN REACH by Sarah Mayberry, available August 2012 from Harlequin® Superromance®.

Harlequin®

ROMANTIC
SUSPENSE

CINDY DEES

takes you on a wild journey to find the truth
in her new miniseries

Code X

Aiden McKay is more than just an ordinary man. As part of
an elite secret organization, Aiden was genetically enhanced
to increase his lung capacity and spend extended time under
water. He is a committed soldier, focused and dedicated
to his job. But when Aiden saves impulsive free spirit
Sunny Jordan from drowning she promptly overturns his
entire orderly, solitary world.

As the danger creeps closer, Adien soon realizes Sunny is the
target…but can he save her in time?

Breathless Encounter

Find out this August!

plus
**BONUS
STORY
INSIDE!**

Look out for a reader-favorite bonus story included in each
Harlequin Romantic Suspense book this August!

HRS27786